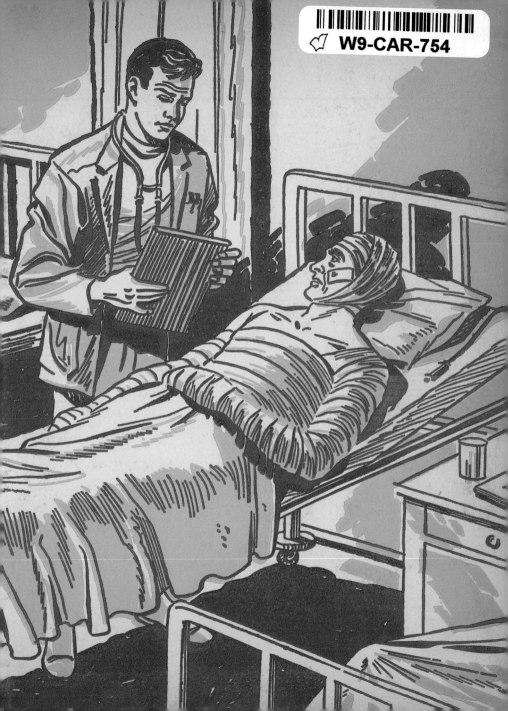

Joann Miller   by: danny Miller - 18
June 14, 1965

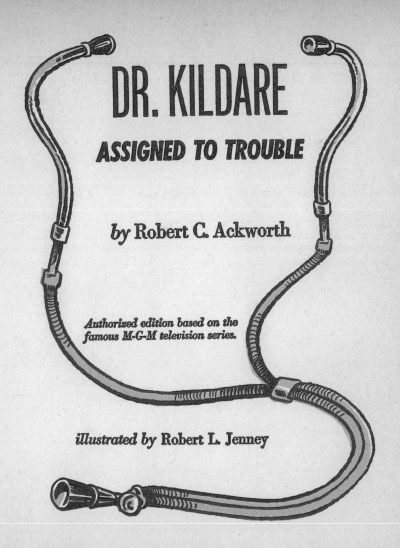

DR. KILDARE

ASSIGNED TO TROUBLE

by Robert C. Ackworth

Authorized edition based on the famous M-G-M television series.

illustrated by Robert L. Jenney

WHITMAN PUBLISHING COMPANY
Racine, Wisconsin

The Dr. Kildare Television Series
is produced by
Arena Productions, Inc.
in association with
Metro-Goldwyn-Mayer Television.

CONTENTS

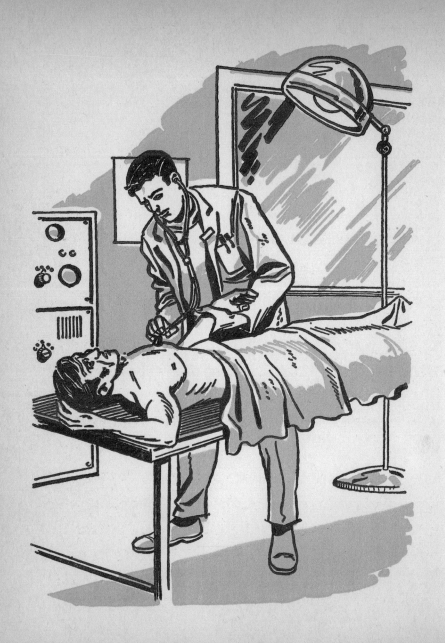

1 *Blair General*

Dr. James Kildare thought he had a coronary on his hands. The thin, flushed, anxious man lay nervously on the examining table in the treatment room as Kildare moved the stethoscope over his chest. The man's face worked and his frown showed anxiety and even hostility. The worst of the man's pain had passed, but Kildare knew he was suffering from something almost as bad—fear that it would strike again.

Kildare straightened up, smiling down at the man in an attempt to calm him, for one of Dr. Gillespie's firm rules was that the doctor must try to reassure the patient. But it did not work in this case. The man glared at Kildare and started to raise himself up on an elbow.

"Why don't you do something for me?" he said

bitterly. "Another attack might be building up in me this very moment."

Gently, Kildare eased the man back down on the table.

"If it does come, we'll be right here to give you immediate help, Mr. Swanson."

But Swanson was not reassured. He still glared, and Kildare could only assume that he was deeply afraid and that his fear made him angry, made him want to lash out at the nearest object, which was Kildare. It was not an uncommon attitude and called for patience and understanding, as Gillespie said.

"I don't think you've given me much help so far," Swanson said. "All you've done is look at me. You haven't done anything."

"We have to find out what's wrong with you first."

Swanson began to push himself up, then slumped back again, obviously exhausted from his ordeal. "You're a *fine* doctor, you are, if you don't know. I'll tell you then. I've had a heart attack."

The nasty tone and unfair attack on Kildare's diagnostic ability almost caused him to lose his composure. But he forced himself to keep calm, for he remembered all too well that time during his first week of internship when a patient like this one had goaded him into losing control and lashing back. It had been the worst of the many mistakes he'd made at Blair General Hospital, and Dr. Gillespie had warned that he did not ever want to hear of Kildare losing his temper in front of a patient again.

"You haven't necessarily had a heart attack, Mr. Swanson," Kildare said calmly. "The pains you had could mean something else, too."

A flicker of light came into Swanson's questioning eyes, crowding out some of the tension of fear hovering in them. "You mean—"

Swanson stopped as the door opened and Dr. Younger, the resident in charge of Admitting

Service, stepped in. Kildare was glad to see him. Younger had the authority to decide on admissions. If Swanson needed to be admitted, having Younger present from the beginning would save time later.

"This is Dr. Younger, Mr. Swanson. He's just as interested in your case as I am." Kildare saw the patient relax a little more—a hopeful sign that he would now be more reasonable. "Let's start at the beginning, Mr. Swanson. You said you had two attacks this morning?"

"Yes," Swanson said in a less surly tone than before. "The first one came right after breakfast when I was going upstairs to get ready for work. It was short, less than a minute, and I didn't pay much attention to it. But then I had another attack when I was walking to work."

"The same kind of pain as the first time?" Kildare asked.

"Yes. It was as if my chest and my shoulder were being crushed by a vise. My left arm, too.

The second attack was twice as bad as the first. A passer-by hailed a police car, and the cops brought me here."

"Ever had any attacks like these before?" Kildare asked.

"No."

"What about palpitations? Or dizziness? Or digestive disturbances?"

"Well, digestive disturbances once in a while the last two years."

"Did you ever see a doctor about them?"

"No, I don't have a doctor. Never had much reason to go to one until now. Doctor, what *is* wrong with me? Have I had a heart attack or not?"

"It may be," Kildare said, "that you've only had a temporary spasm of the blood vessels of the heart rather than a true coronary." He looked at Younger for confirmation, and Younger nodded. "If that's so, then this may be an early sign of impending heart disease."

Swanson sighed. "What's going to happen to me?"

Younger stepped up to the patient with a smile. "Right now you're going to have an electrocardiogram, and then we'll see what's next."

Kildare attached the leads of the electrocardiograph to the patient, and an electrocardiogram was run. A minute later, Younger was studying it while Swanson looked anxiously at him.

Younger turned to the patient. "I'm glad to say that the electrocardiogram shows no damage to your heart, Mr. Swanson. Your trouble was probably caused by a simple spasm, as Dr. Kildare said. But we want to be absolutely sure about this, so we'd like to keep you in the hospital for a few days to do some lab tests and some repeat electrocardiograms to confirm that there's no damage."

"All right, Doctor," Swanson said. "Anything you say."

Kildare smiled to himself. Now that the patient understood the situation better, and now that his

worst fears had been somewhat reduced, his attitude had reversed itself. He would be cooperative
now, and in all probability he would be out of the
hospital all the faster because of it.

A moment later a medical attendant took
Swanson away to put him through the admitting
procedure, and Younger went on to the next treatment room, where one of Kildare's fellow interns
was examining a patient and would need Younger's help. Younger and the assistant residents—
who were responsible for supervising the interns
—had been kept hopping this morning, for the
caseload on Admitting Service had been very
heavy. Kildare had drawn a rich variety of cases,
the more serious among them being a duodenal
ulcer, a fractured ulna, a third degree burn, a hep-
atitis case, and a vertigo victim. Kildare had been
glad for the variety, for it meant broader experience, and he needed experience. He had plenty
of theory behind him from four hard years in
medical school, but he was only in his second

month of applying the theory practically in the wards of Blair General Hospital. And there was still a long road to cover—ten more months of internship, and then the years of residency—before he would reach the goal he had set for himself in childhood.

Kildare walked to the door of the treatment room and looked down the corridor, wondering where his next patient was. There was a flurry of activity out there. People were being ushered into treatment rooms, patients were being wheeled on stretcher carts to the elevators to be taken to the wards, an ambulance was unloading beyond the glass doors at the far end, and the Admitting nurses were busy working on records at their station near the entrance.

An attendant soon brought a new patient to Kildare, a woman complaining of severe stomach pains that she feared might represent an attack of appendicitis. Kildare suspected her trouble might be pancreatitis or a gall bladder attack.

Examination showed that further observation was advisable and a series of tests and X-rays were arranged for the following day. After Kildare reassured the woman and gave her medication to relieve her upset stomach, she was taken back to admissions.

Kildare's next case, a girl of twelve, was not so easy. She was running a high fever of undetermined origin about which her mother was very anxious. Kildare was unable to make a diagnosis even after a thorough examination. Neither was Younger.

"We're going to keep you here for observation, Sally," Younger said, putting his ophthalmoscope back in the breast pocket of his whites after examining the child's reddened eyes. "Don't worry. We'll soon find out what's making you feel bad— and we'll have you back home in no time."

The child smiled and the mother seemed a little less anxious. After they were gone, Younger turned to Kildare.

"Cases like that one remind me that I still have a lot to learn."

Kildare smiled. "We all do."

Younger nodded. "Sure." He looked out the door. "No one seems to be heading this way, Jim. You'd better take this opportunity to stretch your legs. The lull can't last long."

Kildare followed Younger out into the corridor and decided to stroll down and say good morning to Nurse Ashby, something he hadn't had time to do until now because of the avalanche of patients. The veteran Admitting nurse smiled at him when he came up.

"Well, Dr. Kildare, you look happy in spite of the fact that we've been working you exceptionally hard this morning."

Kildare smiled back. "And why not?" he said lightly. "I'm a doctor—which I've wanted to be since I was eight years old. And I'm doing my internship at the best hospital in the city—no, in the state. So why shouldn't I be happy?"

The nurse laughed. "Agreed."

"Then again, I'm also worried," Kildare said, not quite so lightly. "I keep thinking I might not get a residency here next year, and I'd hate to have to go somewhere else for it." Kildare reddened, sorry he had brought up the subject. Nurse Ashby would probably think he should worry about immediate problems instead of disturbing himself about a residency that he could not even apply for until late in the fall.

But Nurse Ashby smiled. "If you weren't worried about a residency from the very beginning, you wouldn't be human, Dr. Kildare. But don't worry too hard. I've a feeling you'll make it with Dr. Gillespie and the Residency Board when the time comes."

Kildare wished he could be so confident. The truth was, he did not think Dr. Leonard Gillespie, the Chief of Staff at Blair, held him in much esteem. Gillespie was an exacting man and had not hesitated to make an issue of small errors

Kildare had made. Kildare had resented his chief's hard approach until he realized that the older doctor's only motive was to try to turn him and all the other interns into better doctors. Gillespie was resolute in his constant efforts to make Blair General Hospital and its staff the best in the city, and he was very likely to make mincemeat of any intern, resident, attending physician, or anyone else working at Blair who did not respect that determination.

"Here comes Dr. Gillespie," Nurse Ashby suddenly said.

Kildare turned. The tall, graying, dignified Chief of Staff was walking toward them, accompanied by a slight and pale but good-looking blond boy of about sixteen. The atmosphere in the corridor had changed, as it always did anywhere that Gillespie made an appearance. All the medical personnel in the vicinity snapped to attention and made certain they were doing what they should be doing, for everyone at Blair knew that Dr. Gillespie's encompassing eyes missed nothing.

"Dr. Kildare," Gillespie said, "I'd like you to meet Tommy Benton, the son of Dr. Richard Benton."

"Hi, Tommy," Kildare said, and smiled. But the boy didn't smile back, and he accepted Kildare's hand only briefly before he sharply withdrew from it. Kildare looked closely at the boy as he lowered his eyes. Kildare could not see the slightest resemblance between the boy's fine-featured face and the big, jutting-jawed face of Dr. Benton that looked down with bold eyes from the huge portrait mounted in Blair's main entrance hall.

"And this is Nurse Ashby, Tommy," Gillespie went on. "If I remember correctly, Miss Ashby was a surgical nurse when your father was Chief of Surgery here."

"You remember correctly, Dr. Gillespie," the nurse said with a slight twinkle in her eyes. She turned to look at the boy. "I'm certainly glad to meet you, Tommy. Your father was a wonderful man, and none of us who worked with him will ever forget him."

Tommy reddened. He nodded slightly but said nothing.

"I'm showing Tommy around the hospital right now," Gillespie said, turning to move off with the boy, then turning back again briefly. "By the way, Dr. Kildare, I'd like to see you in my office this afternoon right after you go off duty."

Kildare waited until Gillespie was out of ear-shot, then frowned at Nurse Ashby. "I wonder what I've done wrong now."

"Maybe nothing. Dr. Gillespie sometimes calls people to his office to tell them they're doing a good job, you know."

Kildare had a feeling Gillespie did not want to see him for that reason, and he knew he was going to be in suspense about this for the rest of the day.

"I know I shouldn't make snap judgments at

first sight," Nurse Ashby said, "but it seemed to me that there was something about Tommy Benton that seemed—well, unfriendly. Or was it just shyness?"

"I thought he was a little strange." Kildare shrugged. "Not that it matters. We'll probably never see him again."

"If he really is unfriendly, then he certainly doesn't take after his father. Dr. Benton was the most cordial man who ever lived, and that was only one of a dozen reasons why he was so popular around here and so much admired everywhere—"

The nurse was interrupted when Younger came up.

"Flood's on again, Jim, and I've got a nice acute tonsillitis awaiting your tender care. No rest for the wicked or for interns, you know."

Dr. Kildare laughed at the joke—which was not really a joke but only a statement of truth—and hurried off to his new patient.

2   *Unexpected Assignment*

Dr. Kildare hurried along the corridor toward the staff cafeteria, feeling a little tired after the morning's activities on the service, but feeling satisfied, too. This was his last week on Admitting Service, and he felt that he was now doing a much better job at diagnosis, and in his general handling of the patients, than he had at the beginning. He hoped that the report Dr. Younger would send about him to Dr. Gillespie would be good.

He turned a corner and bumped into an orderly hurrying toward Hematology with a rack of tubes holding blood specimens to be analyzed. Kildare apologized and walked on, smiling at two second-year student nurses he knew as he passed them down the hall. He had become increasingly aware of the importance of Blair's nursing school ever since Dr. Gillespie had stated in an interns' conference that good nursing was as important to the patient's welfare as was good doctoring.

At the next corner, he paused for a moment, looking down the corridor to General Medicine Service where he was to begin the next phase of his rotating internship starting Monday. He walked on, thinking of how little ground he'd covered at Blair so far in comparison with what he would be expected to accomplish over the whole year. Sometimes he wondered how he would be able to get through it all, but hundreds of Blair interns had borne up under the strain, and Kildare intended doing the same.

Kildare arrived at the cafeteria, went through the line, and was waved down to a table by Dr. Downs, who had the distinction of being the first doctor at Blair to be granted a General Practice residency, which would rotate him through the services during the next two years instead of confining him to one specialty. The other men who greeted Kildare were Dr. Enders and Dr. Ives, both assistant residents in General Surgery.

"We were just talking about Dr. Gillespie," Downs said. "Who would have thought we'd live to see the day when he would be serving as a tour guide through Blair for a teenager?"

Enders laughed. "We wouldn't be seeing that day if the boy weren't Dr. Benton's son. Remember, Benton and Gillespie were great friends in the old days when they were working together to push Blair to top place among the local hospitals."

"Well, they made it, didn't they?" Ives asked. "And let's give Gillespie credit. He doesn't claim to have done it alone."

Kildare agreed silently. The fact was, Gillespie was forever emphasizing Dr. Benton's achievements and underplaying his own. Dr. Benton had been dead for a decade now—he had been killed in a hunting accident—but Dr. Gillespie and Benton's other friends had kept his name so alive that he had become a legend around the hospital.

His imprint was present in tangible ways, too. A rich patient whose life Dr. Benton had saved with his surgical skill had donated, in the doctor's memory, the largest operating amphitheater in the hospital. And the new surgical research pavilion that would soon be constructed was to be named after Dr. Benton.

"Dr. Benton had quite a life even before he came to Blair, you know," Ives said.

Downs smiled. "The Benton story isn't exclusively the property of General Surgery, gentlemen. I happen to know about that tour he did in India as a missionary surgeon after he'd turned down a dozen top offers from New York hospitals. He was in India about ten years, built a hospital from scratch, and was credited with saving hundreds of lives. He didn't leave there until he found a successor capable of finishing the work he'd started."

"And when he returned to the States," Enders said, "he wasn't content just to settle down to a quiet practice. When he wasn't in the operating room, he was barnstorming on his own, giving speeches on the great need for missionary medicine, raising funds for the India hospital."

"A better reason was that he was one of the best surgeons in the country," Ives said.

"You know what the rumor is?" Downs asked. "That the boy is going to spend the rest of the summer here—not as a patient, but just as a guest of the hospital."

Kildare laughed. "I can't think of anything more unlikely. I don't know how such ridiculous rumors get started around here."

But suddenly he was wondering if he might be wrong.

Dr. Kildare stopped to say hello to Susan Deigh, Dr. Gillespie's secretary and one of the prettiest girls around Blair, and then knocked on the great man's door. In a moment Gillespie commanded him to enter. When Kildare went in, Gillespie was studying a case history. After an interminable moment, the older doctor's probing, intelligent eyes moved upward and latched on Kildare, who answered the leveling gaze with a steady one of his own. Kildare had learned that Gillespie did not respect those who could not stand the impact of his withering appraisals.

"Sit down, Dr. Kildare. This will take a while."

That sounded ominous, but Kildare tried to hide his feeling of uneasiness as he sat down.

"I took particular pains to introduce you to Tommy Benton this morning," Gillespie went on, "because you'll be seeing a good deal of him. He'll be with us until late in September, when he will go home for his senior year in high school."

"He will?"

"Admittedly, it's an unusual situation." Gillespie smiled slightly. "I imagine that the rumor factory operating at Blair will make the most of it."

Kildare smiled uncertainly and fidgeted.

"I'm sure," Gillespie said, "you are aware of

what a great man Dr. Benton was. As our Chief
of Surgery he instituted a vast program for devel-
oping the surgical techniques that have made Blair
tops in the field. And, of course, he performed
countless difficult operations in addition to supervising the surgical services. But Dr. Benton was
far too big a man to stop with his responsibilities
in surgery. He was primarily interested in making
Blair a great hospital as a whole. He was a force-
ful man with a bold personality, and he unceas-
ingly used those attributes in the promotion of the
hospital. He literally ground money out of our
board and out of the city for our expansion—at
the expense of other hospitals, I'm afraid. His interests were entirely humanitarian—he wanted
to make this a great hospital answering the needs
of all who came to it. And his interests were as
broad as they were humanitarian. Perhaps you
know that Dr. Benton was responsible for the de-
velopment of our Rehabilitation and Physical
Medicine Service and for the establishment of our

Home Care program for the chronically ill."

Kildare nodded, and he would have frowned if Gillespie had not been looking directly at him. He was growing increasingly uncomfortable from the prolonged suspense.

"I could go on for hours about Dr. Benton's accomplishments," Gillespie said, "but we had better get to the matter of why his son will be with us. When Dr. Benton was killed ten years ago, Mrs. Benton took Tommy away to live in the small town where Dr. Benton was born. Last

winter she wrote me that the boy wanted to follow in his father's footsteps. But since Tommy has been isolated from medical life during his formative years, Mrs. Benton thought he should see things firsthand here at Blair before he made a definite decision on his career. The board decided, in view of Dr. Benton's contributions to the hospital, to let Tommy come in here as an observer." Gillespie smiled. "You might say that Tommy will be a junior intern around here for a while— *your* junior intern, Dr. Kildare."

Kildare could not repress a gasp. "Mine?"

"I intend making you responsible for him, Doctor. For the rest of the week, Tommy will be having a general look at the over-all operations of the hospital, but starting next week, when you begin your tour of General Medicine, he'll be with you most of the time."

"And I'm to be responsible for him?" Kildare frowned. Already he did not like this surprising assignment. Being forced to look after Tommy

Benton would take time and energy Kildare felt he could better devote to getting all he could out of his internship. Besides, he had a feeling from his brief meeting with Tommy Benton this morning that the boy would not be easy to deal with.

"Yes," Gillespie said. "You're here to learn, and so is he. You will teach him all you can—although he will not, of course, be treating patients. His activities will be limited to observation. He understands that you are the person he's to take his questions and problems to—"

"Dr. Gillespie—"

"That will be all, Dr. Kildare. I suggest that you go immediately to Room one-twenty-one in the interns' quarters, where Tommy has been installed. You could begin your friendship by taking him to supper."

Dr. Kildare hesitated, feeling he should argue against this assignment right now. But Dr. Gillespie's tone had warned that the matter was settled. The young intern rose and left the room.

Dr. Kildare walked slowly down the corridor of the interns' quarters, a section of small, plainly furnished rooms known among the staff as Shangri-La. The door of Room 121 was slightly ajar, and Kildare saw Tommy Benton sitting on a chair staring out the window. Kildare knocked and had a smile ready when the boy turned. But Tommy didn't smile back, and he said, "Come in," in a tone that was anything but invitational.

Still, Kildare forced himself to continue his smile. He even tried to make his tone enthusiastic. "Do you remember me, Tommy?"

"Yes." Tommy stared briefly at Kildare, then looked away. "Dr. Gillespie said you'd be looking after me while I'm here."

"Well, not exactly looking after you. You're too old for that." Kildare paused, expecting some sort of response, but there was none. "How about eating supper with me, Tommy, so we can get started knowing each other?"

"All right," Tommy said coldly.

The boy rose, and they went out. As they walked down the corridor, Kildare tried asking a few questions about Tommy's background, but he barely got blunt "yes" and "no" answers. Long before they reached the staff cafeteria, Kildare was wondering how they would ever get through a whole meal together if they could not sustain conversation for the few minutes it took to reach the cafeteria from the interns' quarters.

In the cafeteria, Kildare decided to try to share the burden. Two of his best friends among the interns—Dr. Adam Franks and Dr. Floyd Harriman—were just beginning supper at one of the roomier tables. They were both good at getting things going and keeping them light. So when Kildare and Tommy had their trays filled, Kildare steered the boy over to their table.

"Glad to know you, Tommy," Harriman said, offering a firm hand that Tommy disposed of quickly. "We just heard a rumor that you're here to learn all about us. The first thing you'll learn is that we have more rumors than anything else."

Tommy didn't laugh. He didn't even smile as he sat down.

"Hope you'll like it here with us, Tommy," Franks said. "Maybe as Dr. Benton's son you'll have enough influence to see that improvements are made at Blair—such as more money and more sleep for the interns."

The joke fell flat, as did the next two that Harriman and Franks tried. Then Kildare tried shop talk, but that wakened no response from Tommy, so he led the conversation consecutively from the baseball clubs' current standings to the latest missile attempt to the newest Hollywood comedy. Tommy was interested in none of it. He sat stolidly and scarcely ate anything. When they were only halfway through their meals, Tommy shoved his plate back and rose, saying he wasn't hungry and was going to his room to read.

Kildare smiled with strain. "I'm in one-eighteen, just a few doors from you, Tommy. I'm on call tonight, and I'll be in my room. Drop down for a chat, will you?"

"All right," Tommy said, then wheeled and walked away.

Harriman waited until Tommy was out of earshot and then said, "Any chat you have with that young man, Jim, will be strictly one-sided."

"He's a peculiar one, all right," Franks said.

"Let's not draw any conclusions until we know him better," Kildare said, although he was aware that he had privately drawn some quick conclusions on Tommy Benton himself.

"Frankly, I'm not a bit interested in knowing him any better," Harriman said. "Cold ones like Tommy leave me exactly that—*cold*."

Dr. Kildare frowned. He could imagine the ribbing he was going to take from Harriman and Franks, and others, when they found out about his assignment. He wished there were some way he could bow out of it right now—for the more he thought about it, the less he liked it.

3

A Bad Start

The alarm shattered Dr. Kildare's sleep, bolting him into wakefulness. He was frowning before he got the clock shut off. This wasn't a good way to start the day, feeling tired and angry, but he was feeling both ways—tired because he had lain awake late thinking about his unwanted assignment, angry because Tommy had not dropped in to talk last evening as he had said he would. The worst part was, the boy had left the hospital for the evening without a word to Kildare.

Kildare staggered out of bed, feeling as groggy as if he'd just been roused in the middle of the night to handle a case, as he had been last night. He wished he could have those precious few minutes of half-sleep he usually stole after the alarm went off, but he couldn't this morning.

Much as he disliked the idea, he had to get Tommy Benton started, and he was allowing himself an extra half hour for it.

He was a little surprised to find Tommy up and waiting for him, dressed in the uniform he'd been provided, the standard whites worn by all the male medical personnel at Blair. In the uniform, the boy would not stand out noticeably on the wards. His serious, worried expression made him look older than sixteen, but he nevertheless looked too young to be mistaken for an intern. Kildare judged that most patients would probably think Tommy was one of the medical attendants employed by the hospital.

"Did you have a good night's sleep?" Kildare asked after he had greeted Tommy.

"I guess so," Tommy said, moving toward the door. "Let's go. We've got a lot to cover, don't we? So we'd better get started."

Kildare almost frowned at the boy's hostile tone and negative beginning. He would do better to begin by apologizing for not showing up for that talk with Kildare last evening. But Kildare decided that nothing would be gained from making an issue of that at this point.

"Yes, let's go," Kildare said. "Last evening Dr. Gillespie's office sent over your schedule for this week. We can discuss it at breakfast."

Again, the walk to the cafeteria was an uncomfortable one. When they were seated with their breakfast trays, Kildare ended the silence by getting to the business at hand. The memorandum from Dr. Gillespie had suggested that a general indoctrination would make a logical beginning.

"As you may know, Tommy," Kildare began, "Blair General is the second largest hospital in the state. We serve a metropolitan population of a half million and a surrounding suburban population of over a million. We are a teaching hospital. We have a large nursing school. We have the finest facilities and finest equipment of any hospital in the state, and we keep constantly up-to-

date with the most modern methods in all services. We have a big staff. It takes more workers
to take care of the patients than there are patients
themselves. Blair has sixty-one interns and residents, a hundred and fifty attending physicians
and surgeons, ninety-three nurses, more than a
hundred nurse's aides and volunteer workers, and
hundreds of medical attendants and technicians
and service workers—"

Kildare stopped. Tommy was staring off into
space, apparently lost in his thoughts.

"Look, Tommy," Kildare said irritably, "I'm
not talking because I'm fascinated with the sound
of my own voice. I'm supposed to teach you something about Blair, and you're supposed to listen.
Or maybe you're just not interested."

Kildare immediately regretted his tone and his
words, for he knew Dr. Gillespie would consider
this a childish outburst unworthy of a Blair doctor, and he would be right. He saw Tommy look
at him, and this time the boy's eyes hovered on

him instead of turning away immediately as they usually did. Tommy had deep brown eyes, and they seemed to be full of unanswered questions. There was a touch of sadness in them, too.

"Sure, I'm interested," the boy said in a strange voice. "My father practically made this hospital what it is today—so naturally I'm interested."

Kildare hesitated. The boy was taking an exaggerated view of his father's achievements at Blair, wonderful though they were, and Kildare did not quite know how to handle it.

"Your father did a great deal for Blair," he said, "but he didn't do it entirely alone—"

"My father," Tommy interrupted in a harsh tone, "was a very big man in all ways. He was a hero. *Everybody* looked up to him. At home they still talk about the big things he did with his life. A great surgeon, a great humanitarian—they're always saying that about him. You make it sound as if he was—well, hardly anything."

"I certainly didn't mean it that way," Kildare

said quickly. "Your father was a very important man. My point is that no individual man is entirely responsible for what Blair is today. This hospital—in fact the whole hospital system—is constructed on the contributions to progress made by a lot of different men over a period of many years. The same thing goes for the medical and surgical knowledge we have today. What is it but the sum total of what a lot of men have learned and passed on to us over a long period of time?"

"I suppose that's true," Tommy said reluctantly, "but I want you to understand that my father was *really* important." He paused. "Go on. Let's get this lecture over with."

Kildare frowned. This boy seemed absolutely determined to make Kildare dislike him. "There won't be any more lecture, Tommy. Eat your breakfast, and I'll take you to your first service."

A few minutes later, Kildare led Tommy on a long and silent walk through the corridors to Pediatrics, where he left him in the care of the smiling resident, Dr. Emmy Lorfield, a very friendly young woman who had made a happy choice for herself when she had decided to become a children's doctor.

As he left the service, Dr. Kildare wondered how long it would take for the sullen Tommy Benton to cause Dr. Lorfield to stop smiling.

As Dr. Emmy Lorfield said to Dr. Kildare at lunch in the staff cafeteria that noon, she hadn't found the morning spent with Tommy Benton to be a very agreeable experience, and had been glad enough to turn the boy over to the resident of Orthopedics just before noon.

"It wasn't that he was really nasty. It was more that he was—well, negative." Dr. Lorfield frowned. "Frankly, from what I've heard about Dr. Benton, it's hard to believe that this boy is his son."

During the next few days, Kildare heard simi-lar things about Tommy Benton from other doc-

tors, most of whom were much bolder in their ex-
pressions of dislike for Tommy than the gentle
Emmy Lorfield had been.

"He's just a plain awful kid," Harriman said,
after being saddled with Tommy during the boy's
half-day tour of Anesthesiology. "Surly, uncom-
municative, uncooperative, and unlikeable."

Kildare tried hard to make a friend of Tommy,
though he did not like the idea of trying to force
friendship on someone who did not want it. But
Kildare had to try, for this was duty. He did not
mention to Tommy the unfavorable things he had
heard about him around the hospital. He tried
to make a positive approach, tried to make the
boy feel he was really interested in him and
wanted to know him better.

But Tommy resisted Kildare's efforts, and during the meals they ate together that week, Kildare
was able to learn only a few things about the boy,
such as that Tommy and his mother lived in the
old house his father had been born in and that

Tommy had a slight interest in entomology. That interest seemed a little mild for the son of a great surgeon, but Kildare was glad enough to learn that Tommy had any interests at all. But when he tried to probe deeper, Tommy shut him off.

"Look, Dr. Kildare, what I've done in the past has nothing to do with what I'm doing here."

Nothing Kildare tried did any good. Tommy was just as stiff with him at the end of the week as he had been at the beginning. On Friday, Kildare came to a reluctant decision. When he went off duty, he went straight to Dr. Gillespie and asked to be released from the responsibility of looking after Tommy. He did not mention the bad impression Tommy had made around the hospital. Gillespie would have heard about that anyway.

"I don't think I'm qualified to handle him," Kildare said. "I can't get close to him. He just doesn't seem to like me."

Gillespie focused his penetrating eyes on Kildare. "I'm surprised that you're prepared to give up so easily on this."

"For the boy's own good, it would be better if you put another intern in charge of him."

"I'm quite sure," Gillespie said icily, "that in trying to evade this assignment you're thinking of your own good rather than Tommy's. Your request is refused, Dr. Kildare." Gillespie frowned. "I'm not unaware, Doctor, that Tommy has not been well liked around Blair thus far. All right then, the boy is difficult and represents a challenge. You should welcome it. A doctor should be able to deal effectively with all kinds of people —including difficult teenagers. If he can't, he isn't a good doctor. Remember that when you're dealing with Tommy Benton."

Dr. Kildare left Dr. Gillespie's office feeling low. Not only had he failed to have himself relieved of the burden that was Tommy Benton. Worse yet, he had displeased Dr. Gillespie again. And he could not afford it.

4 *Dangerous Ground*

When Dr. Kildare arrived at the nurses' station on General Medicine Wednesday morning, Nurse Joyner, the head nurse of the service, smiled cheerfully at him and then looked over his shoulder and down the corridor.

"Where's your shadow this morning, Doctor?"

Kildare shrugged. "I don't know. He wasn't in his room when I stopped for him before breakfast."

"Maybe he's gone over the hill," the nurse said with a laugh. "That's what they call it in the Army, isn't it?"

"Oh, I don't think he's run away," Kildare said, smiling with strain. He'd been surprised to find Tommy's room empty this morning, but he wasn't alarmed. He suspected that Tommy was only trying to annoy him.

"Frankly," the nurse said, "we can hope he *has* left us, Dr. Kildare."

Kildare didn't comment. He didn't need to. In just two days, Tommy Benton had managed to incur the dislike of most of the medical personnel on this service.

But right now Kildare did not have time to worry about it. He had duties to perform before rounds were made. He asked Nurse Joyner for the order books for Wards G and H and took them and the portable chart rack, containing a chart for every person on both wards, into the small ward office, where he could usually work without disturbance.

In there he checked the order sheets to make certain they had all been brought up to date. He checked to see that laboratory reports had been made and recorded on the appropriate charts, for all tests ordered. An especially large number of laboratory tests had been made yesterday because of an unusually large influx of new patients in General Medicine. In preparation for rounds, Kildare familiarized himself with the laboratory results. He was just finishing looking at the last chart when Dr. Udell, the assistant resident in charge of Wards G and H, opened the door and stepped in. He handed a clipboard containing some admitting forms—blank except for the name Zimmer—to Kildare.

"When you get a minute, get this history, will you, Jim? The patient's in the third unit, Ward G. He came in through Emergency last night. He was so uncomfortable from nausea and from bringing up blood that they rushed him onto the ward without finishing the admitting details." Udell paused. "Where's golden boy?"

"I don't know. Maybe he's decided to spend his days away from Blair as he does his evenings. I'll admit that I'm curious about where he goes. He couldn't have made friends this quickly."

"Is he the type to make friends anyway?" Udell

asked. "Do you know what the nurses on this service are calling him? Mr. Sour."

"He's certainly not making friends and influencing people very fast."

"I can't figure out why that boy wants to be a doctor. Oh, I know it takes all types in our field— but that type, no."

"I don't think he does want to be a doctor," Kildare said.

"You don't? Then what's he doing here? And why has this special program been set up for him?"

"The program has been set up because his father did a great deal for Blair. As to why Tommy's here when he doesn't really want to be— well, I don't think he knows yet that he doesn't want to be a doctor."

"Now you're confusing me."

"It's just a theory, of course, but I think Tommy's general attitude toward all of us simply indicates that inside him he doesn't want to be involved in this at all—although he would probably be the first to deny it."

"If your theory's true," Udell said, "I hope he wises up soon and saves himself and the rest of us a lot of unnecessary trouble of going on with this program." Udell turned to go out, then looked back. "First rounds will be a few minutes late. Dr. Murray is in Pathology seeing about some rush lab tests."

Udell went out, and Kildare followed after looking at his watch. Tommy was now almost a half hour late, and by all rights Kildare should report the matter to Gillespie without delay. But he decided to wait five minutes more. He returned the order books to Nurse Joyner.

The nurse smiled. "I'm always glad to see the order books back where they belong. One day last year an intern happened to have the order books in his hands when he was summoned outside the hospital on a personal emergency—I believe it was that his father was in an automobile accident. Anyway, he was so frightened about it that he didn't notice that he carried the order books right out with him. For several hours, until they came back to us, things were in a state of high confusion here. It cannot be said that we nurses knew what we were doing during that period."

Kildare laughed and so did Nurse Joyner, but he was certain that the nurse had not thought the situation of the missing books funny at the time it had happened since those order sheets contained complete instructions to the nurses on the care of the patients, and without them the nurses would be helpless.

Tommy suddenly arrived, a little breathlessly, and Kildare glanced at the clock over the elevators. The boy was thirty-five minutes late.

"I have a good excuse. I had a headache when I got up—so I thought I'd better take a walk and try to get rid of it."

"It would only have taken you a minute to stop and tell me."

"I didn't think you'd care."

Kildare's fists clenched at his sides. Maybe it was true that Tommy had awakened with a headache and had gone for a walk to get rid of it. But it was probably also true that he had failed to warn Kildare that he was doing it just to annoy him. The boy seemed to be asking for trouble again. It was as if he were daring Kildare to lose patience with him. Indeed, Kildare did feel like telling Tommy a few pointed things, but a display of temper would only prove to Tommy that he had succeeded in annoying him.

"Come along," Kildare said in a deceptively calm voice, turning and heading toward Ward G, the home of General Medicine's men patients. "I'm going to take a patient's history. This will be new for you, so I expect you to pay close attention."

They entered Ward G and passed a few small one-bed rooms in the first section of the ward where critically ill patients were kept in complete privacy until their conditions improved to the point where they could be moved in with other patients. When they entered the next section— which contained six beds that could be closed off from one another by curtains when privacy was needed—the usual early-morning activities were proceeding. A volunteer worker was distributing books from a book cart, and another volunteer was carrying off breakfast trays. A nurse was giving medication to an elderly man, and a nurse's aide was stripping down a bed just vacated by a discharged patient. At the rear of this section, a nursing instructor was demonstrating the pulse-and-temperature-taking procedure to a group of six student nurses gathered around a patient's bed.

Similar activities were going on in the next section, and here, as had happened a moment ago in the first section, several patients nodded and said good morning to Kildare as he and Tommy passed through. Kildare was pleased that a good number of the patients were already getting to know him even though he had only been on this service for two days.

"Looks as if you're making friends," Tommy said.

"I hope so," Kildare said. "Dr. Gillespie feels that making a friend of the patient is half the battle, and I agree with him. Most patients enter here full of fears—fear that they aren't going to get well, fear of unfamiliar routines and strange faces, fear of tests and examinations. A continuation of those fears can slow down a patient's recovery. So if the doctor can make a friend of the patient and allay his fears, everyone gains." Kildare looked at Tommy. "The most successful doctors are the ones that like people—all kinds of people."

Tommy frowned. "What's that supposed to mean?"

"Just what I said. A doctor has to gain the confidence of his patients before he can help them, and he can't gain their confidence unless he shows that he likes them."

"What about the doctor being liked by the patients?" Tommy asked, surprisingly. "Shouldn't it work both ways?"

"Yes, of course." Kildare looked at the unsmiling boy again. If Tommy understood these things, and intended trying to model himself after his father, then why didn't he apply a little of this philosophy to himself and make himself more likeable?

"My father," Tommy said, "had plenty of friends. Patients, doctors, nurses, everybody. Everybody respected him."

"Yes, of course," Kildare said just as they arrived at Mr. Zimmer's bed at the end of the ward. The thin, pale, middle-aged man smiled warily when Kildare sat down beside his bed with the clipboard in his hand. Kildare smiled at him. "I'm Dr. Kildare, Mr. Zimmer. How are you feeling?"

"I feel a lot better now, Doctor, but I sure felt terrible when they brought me in here. I had this attack a couple of hours after supper last night—a lot of blood coming up and some bad pains in my stomach. I felt dizzy, too, and I could hardly make it over to my neighbor—thought I was going to blank out. My neighbor called a policeman. The policeman sent for an ambulance, and the first thing I knew, I was being taken care of downstairs. When I woke up this morning, I found myself in bed here, and I felt a lot better. How long will I be staying?"

"We won't know until we find out a little more about you. You weren't feeling well enough last night to give us your medical history, Mr. Zimmer. It's important that we have this information. In many cases it makes diagnosis easier."

"Well, I've had attacks like last night's in the past, Doctor—but just little ones."

Mr. Zimmer described the attacks and other illnesses, and Kildare noted them in detail.

"I wasn't overestimating the importance of getting an accurate medical history from the patient," Kildare said as he and Tommy walked out. "Illness is often a cumulative thing. In Mr. Zimmer's case, he's been having these attacks— the bringing up of blood, accompanying nausea —for the last year. My guess is he has a stomach ulcer. The point is, knowing what we do about his medical history, we may be able to pinpoint the trouble with only a couple of tests instead of a large number. That way, a lot of time and expense will be saved."

Kildare looked over at Tommy. The boy was staring into space as he walked, apparently not hearing a word Kildare said. All right then, Kildare thought. He had tried. But he wasn't going to waste his breath talking to unlistening ears.

When Kildare and Tommy reached the nurses' station, Dr. Murray, the resident, had just arrived on the service. Murray was a good and efficient doctor who allowed no wasting of time, so rounds began immediately. They proceeded through Ward H, which housed Medicine's women patients, and then through Ward G, which housed the men patients. They stopped at each bed in each ward. Kildare was pushing the portable chart rack, and he handed each patient's chart to Murray to review just before Murray examined the patient. Murray was a tough and exacting man when he dealt with the interns he supervised, but he was reassuringly gentle with the patients. After he finished with a patient, and before he proceeded to the next bed, he would record any necessary changes on the patient's chart and would tell Kildare of any changes he was to make on the order sheet regarding the nurse's instructions. Quite often, too, he would ask Kildare questions about the case at hand and would readily point it out when the answers were wrong or incomplete.

After the rounds, Murray left for a clinical conference, and Tommy said to Kildare, "He treated you like a worm every time you made a wrong answer." The boy seemed almost pleased.

"You're wrong, Tommy. He was only doing his job—driving it home to me that I've got a lot to learn. Do you know what the original meaning of the title 'doctor' was? It meant 'teacher.' When Dr. Murray questions me, and then criticizes me for making incorrect answers, it's only part of the teaching process. As the resident, Dr. Murray is responsible for teaching the interns and the assistant residents under him. He's tough, but he has to be tough. He's responsible to the chief of the service for how things go on these wards—both with us and the patients. In turn, the chief of the service is responsible to Dr. Gillespie."

"Everybody's responsible to somebody around here. What is this—a hospital or the Army?"

"Maybe it is a little like the Army. But there must be discipline and a setting down of responsibilities here if we're going to save lives and get people cured and keep mistakes at a minimum."

"I think it's creepy. Somebody always watching you, just waiting to pounce on you."

"We don't take that attitude. We keep remembering we're here to learn."

Tommy lapsed into silence then, after this unusual outburst of comments, and he was completely quiet during the next hour while they went through the wards and Kildare changed the dressings of patients who needed them. Every time Kildare glanced at Tommy during this tour, he found the boy looking away absently.

It was little better during the following hour, when Kildare and Udell, the assistant resident, checked the new admissions. Tommy seemed little interested in the new cases, which covered the usual variety coming on the Medicine wards. They included a stroke victim, a diabetic, an ulcer sufferer, a coronary patient, a cirrhosis case, and a burn victim. The latter, a big man named Henry Reeves, was a new admission to the ward, not to the hospital. For several days he had been hovering near death from shock and third degree burns in the Intensive Care Unit, where patients were kept under constant watch night and day. Kildare had heard about his tragic case. A fire in his home had wiped out his family. Reeves had almost died trying to save them.

Kildare and Udell worked up order sheets covering treatment procedures, medications, diet, and laboratory tests for each new admission—the orders being subject to later modification by Dr. Murray when he examined the patients. When they were finished, the morning had vanished, and so had Tommy Benton, without a word.

Kildare walked to the staff cafeteria for lunch feeling a little angry. It wasn't that he expected Tommy Benton to eat lunch with him, for of course they needed a break from each other at the middle of the day. But why couldn't Tommy find it within himself to be a little polite and say "See you after lunch, Dr. Kildare" or almost anything else instead of simply vanishing.

This wasn't working out at all, and Dr. Kildare wished he knew what to do about it.

Tommy was twelve minutes late returning from lunch and offered no explanation. Dr. Kildare was irritated, but he didn't make an issue of the matter, one reason being that he didn't have time. They were going to have a busy afternoon.

First there were rounds during which Dr. Murray examined the new patients, generally approving the orders the assistant resident had drawn up for them with Kildare's help. Hardly was that finished when Dr. Trager, the attending physician in charge of General Medicine Service, arrived to conduct teaching rounds. Dr. Trager was an internist with a large outside practice, and he was an excellent lecturer. The learning group today included Dr. Murray, the assistant residents and interns on the service, two nurses, and

Tommy Benton. Dr. Trager would select a patient, and Dr. Murray would read the chart to him, after which Dr. Trager would examine the patient, point out the interesting facets of the case, ask questions of the group, and then answer their questions. When they were halfway through the tour, Dr. Gillespie joined it, observing quietly.

"Are you enjoying your stay with us so far, Tommy?" Gillespie asked after the clinical critique.

"Sure, it's swell, Dr. Gillespie. I'm learning a lot."

Tommy smiled stiffly, and Gillespie smiled back at him.

At the end of the day Dr. Kildare wondered, as he often did, where the time had vanished. It seemed only minutes ago that his clanging alarm clock had started him on this day. It had been a typical day—rounds, admissions, teaching rounds, a clinical conference, and more rounds— but it had been exciting despite the fact that nothing really unusual had happened. All days at Blair, typical or atypical, were exciting.

Kildare was glad about his lot, and he was thinking about that when Tommy Benton made his jarring remark as they walked toward the interns' quarters to get ready for supper.

"Time sure drags around this place," Tommy said in a bitter tone. "I didn't think today was ever going to come to an end."

That remark, Kildare thought, was certainly

undeniable evidence of the complete contrast in attitude and interests between Tommy Benton and himself. But Kildare did not comment at the moment. He waited until they were finishing supper in the staff cafeteria, sitting at a remote corner table alone since the other interns had made it plain to Kildare that they did not consider it a pleasure to have Tommy Benton forced upon them at mealtime.

"Tommy, you mentioned how time dragged for you today. If one day drags for you, what would years of this do to you? Have you ever added up all the time involved in becoming a doctor? Four years of college, four years of medical school, a year of internship, and then, except for those who go directly into general practice or a non-practicing medical job, two to five years of residency in a specialized field—five years in the case of surgery. If you're going to be a surgeon, you're going to spend fourteen years just getting to the point where your career will really begin. That's a lot of time. It's time well spent if a man really wants what he's aiming for. But if he doesn't, if he finds time dragging—"

"I didn't mean it that way," Tommy interrupted. "Time drags because all I'm allowed to do is observe. I can't *do* anything."

"But if what we're doing here at Blair really interested you, time wouldn't drag for you even though you're just observing."

"It does interest me." Tommy sounded angry.

"Are you sure, Tommy? You want to be absolutely sure about it before you invest all that time I was talking about. Becoming a doctor involves so many sacrifices that a man is a fool to try for it unless he wants it more than just about anything else in life."

"I *do* want it more than anything else! But you'd like to talk me out of it because you don't want to bother with me, right?"

"You're completely wrong. It's just that I don't feel we can do you any good—or you us—unless you're absolutely convinced you really want to go on with this program—"

Kildare had no chance to finish. Tommy got up and left the table without a backward glance. For a moment Kildare was angry about the boy's abrupt departure. But then it occurred to him that perhaps he had approached the matter too bluntly. Later that evening he went to Tommy's room, hoping the boy's anger would have diminished and they could talk reasonably. But Tommy had gone out, and Kildare didn't see him until the next morning. Kildare immediately apologized for having upset Tommy yesterday, but Tommy did not accept the apology graciously.

"You just do your job of teaching me, and I'll do mine of listening to you. And we won't discuss anything that isn't absolutely necessary."

Tommy was especially sullen that day, and even more so on Friday. Jim Kildare tried to pretend he didn't notice at all, but he found it more and more difficult to hide his own resentment.

Dr. Gillespie called Dr. Kildare to his office Friday evening right after Kildare went off duty.

"First of all," Gillespie said, "you won't need to go into your difficulties with Tommy Benton. I've heard enough to know that his attitude is still not good, and I realize that it has become an open question of whether or not we were justified in setting up this special program for him. Furthermore, I was quite aware that the enthusiasm Tommy expressed for it to me after the conference on Wednesday had a false ring to it."

"Dr. Gillespie, Tommy and I had a little trouble. I intimated that deep inside him he doesn't really want to be a doctor, and he got angry."

"I should think he would."

"But he should have been glad for me to point out the truth to him."

"People seldom are," Gillespie said. "But aside from that, at this early stage, you had no right to make an assumption like that."

"But Dr. Gillespie, everything points to it—

his hostility, his lack of attention, everything. I thought I'd try to save him time and trouble—and save it for us, too—by showing him the truth."

"You don't know that it *is* true. You jumped to a conclusion without giving the matter enough time and thought. Tommy's attitude could be the result of a dozen different things. It might be a simple nervous reaction to being thrust suddenly into a completely adult world where he doesn't know quite how to handle himself. If so, adjustments will take time and understanding. Apparently you're unwilling to give him either."

Kildare flushed. Perhaps he had made mistakes with the boy.

"I'm sorry I've failed, Dr. Gillespie. But it's difficult to try to guide someone who doesn't want to be guided by you. Tommy and I have been together all week. Instead of growing more at ease with each other, we've grown more uncomfortable with each other. He doesn't like me, and he isn't going to like me, no matter what I do—"

"Stop right there." Gillespie was scowling. "You were leading up to asking again to be relieved of this assignment. Save your breath. I suggest that you stop thinking so much about your difficulties with Tommy and spend your energies finding ways to improve the relationship. And stop rushing into things. In this case you seem to have forgotten that patience is a prime quality a good doctor must have—a quality he must show in both his professional and personal relationships. That will be all, Dr. Kildare."

Dr. Kildare left Dr. Gillespie's office feeling considerably deflated. He had overstepped with the older doctor, and now Gillespie would be watching him more closely than ever. This assignment seemed to have become a kind of personal test of Dr. Kildare's ability to turn an impossible human relationship into an acceptable one. He frowned. He was afraid that if he failed with Tommy Benton, it would affect his future at Blair General Hospital to a considerable extent.

6 *Tommy's Goal*

Tommy Benton went home for the weekend, and for two days Jim Kildare's stresses and strains were confined to those arising from his duties around the hospital—stresses and strains he considered minor in comparison to those he had suffered in his dealings with Tommy. Kildare took a lot of ribbing over the weekend from Harriman and Franks and several nurses about his relationship with his "protégé," as Tommy Benton was now being described. Kildare shrugged it all off with a laugh, but he did not think it was funny, and he was not looking forward to Tommy's return to the hospital.

Tommy was on the service promptly on Monday morning, thereby sparing Kildare the necessity of starting the week off with a reprimand.

But it got started badly anyway. Tommy was even colder to Kildare than he had been last week—probably, Kildare thought, because he still resented that attempt at a heart-to-heart talk. Kildare did not make the same mistake this week. He was as formal as Tommy was.

Tommy was much more alert this week. He seemed determined to give Kildare no opportunity to criticize him. He was always on the service when he was supposed to be, and when Kildare popped questions to see how much Tommy had absorbed, the boy more often than not came forth with the right answers. It would have been fine to report to Dr. Gillespie that Tommy was now making definite progress, but Kildare did not believe that Tommy's heart was really in it.

And the boy was still sullen. He made a quick retreat when any of the doctors or nurses tried to be friendly with him, and most of them soon stopped trying. Tommy Benton's reputation had been firmly established around the hospital.

Even some of the patients had noticed the boy's sullenness and had complained that they did not feel comfortable when he was around. One exception was the burn victim, Henry Reeves, who lay in his bed swathed in bandages. Reeves—who had been numb with sorrow, as a result of the loss of his family—actually showed enough interest in his present surroundings one day to ask Tommy who he was. Kildare was surprised when Tommy responded in a friendly manner to the big man and even stayed at Reeves's bed to visit awhile.

Tommy surprised Kildare even more that evening by showing up at his room. Tommy invariably spent his evenings away from Blair, although Kildare still had no idea where he went and what he did.

"Just what does Dr. Gillespie's job really amount to?" Tommy asked.

Kildare was not so much surprised at the question as he was at the fact that Tommy was asking.

"Dr. Gillespie's job is the biggest in the hospital. He's the head of Blair General, and everything that implies."

"In other words, *he* decides everything that goes on here."

"Well, not everything. The board of directors decides the major policies. Of course, Dr. Gillespie is on the board as the representative of the medical staff—so he pulls his weight with making the policies, too."

"What else does he do?"

"He supervises the financial arrangements of the hospital—a very important item since it costs so much to run Blair. Then, too, he's responsible for interviewing and selecting the medical personnel, though he has help from committees in deciding on the interns and residents. He also has to settle personal problems that can't be handled on lower levels. He handles certain special medical cases himself, too—and he's responsible for seeing that new materials and drugs and mechanical equipment are tested. He conducts some of the teaching rounds. He is constantly checking to see that things are functioning as they should on all levels—from the wards to the clinics to the kitchen."

"Do you think you'll be the head of a big hospital some day?"

Kildare laughed. "It's unlikely. I've never thought about it."

"You haven't? That's surprising. I would have thought you'd have been thinking about your future all along."

"I have been. Ever since I was a boy I've wanted to be a doctor—as good a one as my capabilities will allow. But the chances are unlikely that I'll ever be another Dr. Gillespie or have a job like his. Not impossible, but unlikely. For every big man in the field, there are a thousand little ones. That doesn't mean the little ones don't do important jobs. And the big ones couldn't get along without the little ones."

Tommy walked to the window and looked out,

with his back to Kildare. "I know what I'm going to be," he said over his shoulder. "A big man. Like Dr. Gillespie is. Like my father was."

"That's a worthy ambition, Tommy," Kildare said carefully. "I hope you make it."

"I will," the boy said, again over his shoulder. "I think a man can be what he wants to be—if he wants it badly enough."

"That's true in a lot of cases, Tommy, but not all. Some men just aren't up to reaching the goals they set for themselves."

Tommy turned and looked at Kildare with anger flaring from his brown eyes. "Are you saying I won't reach mine?"

"No. I'm not sure what you can or can't do, Tommy. But I'd be willing to bet that whether you get there or not will depend a lot on how honest your motive is."

"Honest? I don't know what you mean."

Kildare hesitated. Perhaps he was treading on too dangerous ground and should stop now. But he decided that he had to finish what he had started. It would not be fair to dangle Tommy in midair.

"Whether you really want it for yourself—in which case it is an honest motive—or whether you want it because your father was a famous surgeon and you think you ought to be one, too— which is not an honest motive, in my opinion."

"I want it for myself," Tommy said angrily.

"All right," Kildare said, although he was not convinced of Tommy's sincerity. "If that's true, you have a lot in your favor. Getting to the top will depend a lot on you—on how hard you work to develop your potentialities and how much you're willing to sacrifice to make your goal. But getting there will also depend on the help other people give you along the way. I would advise you to think about that—"

Kildare was interrupted when his room phone rang. He'd noticed that Tommy's face had darkened when he had begun to give him advice on his personality problem. The boy seemed relieved at the interruption, and Kildare decided he would drop the matter for the time being. It was enough that things had improved enough between them for Tommy to come to his room to talk this way.

Dr. Ogden, the chief medical resident, was on the phone. He was looking for a doctor to cover for an intern who had been suddenly taken ill on Emergency. Kildare was elected.

"Why don't you come along for an hour or so, Tommy?" Kildare said after he had explained that he had to report for duty right away. "You'd probably find it interesting. Emergency gets some pretty exciting cases—ones that require quick thinking and fast action and are a real test."

Tommy hesitated, and for a long moment Kildare thought he was going to refuse and go off to wherever he usually spent his evenings. But he said, "Yes," and a moment later the two of them were walking side by side to Emergency Service.

7 *Emergency*

Dr. Kildare found that his name had already been chalked in under "Interns on Call" on the duty blackboard at the nurses' station in Emergency. He introduced Tommy to Nurse Potter, the Emergency night-charge nurse, Dr. Cassell, assistant resident in charge, and Dr. Long, the other intern on Emergency duty tonight. Kildare was sorry to see that the boy was distant and cool toward them.

"You arrived during a lull," Cassell said, "but don't be hopeful that it will last long. You know how it is with us here—feast or famine."

"We had a nice insulin shock case about an hour ago," Long said. "A woman of about fifty who was found unconscious in her house by her daughter. She was rushed here, and I immediately proceeded to make my sixth mistake of the day. I diagnosed insulin coma instead of shock. Good thing Dr. Cassell was around to correct me."

Cassell smiled. "If I hadn't, somebody else would have before treatment started. When you think about it, we've got a neat bunch of checks on one another's mistakes around here. We're all watching one another, and the labs are watching all of us." He laughed. "Besides, I'm an assistant resident. As such, I'm good at recognizing interns' mistakes because I made exactly the same ones last year when *I* was an intern."

"It's good to hear an assistant resident admit he was once a human being," Long said.

Everyone laughed except Tommy. Kildare was now beginning to think the boy was incapable of responding to any joke.

"And," Nurse Potter put in, "as Dr. Gillespie was once supposed to have said, a doctor can hardly be considered fit to treat human beings unless he was once a human being himself."

Everyone laughed again—except Tommy.

"Dr. Gillespie should have dropped in here last night on one of his inspection tours," Long said. "It would have delighted him how hard we were working."

"Yes, last night was a flood," Nurse Potter said. "We had almost as much business as we have at the end of a holiday weekend—nosebleeds, burns, fractures, a cardiac standstill, a thyroid crisis, a ptomaine poisoning, a dog bite, a hit-and-run case, a child who ran a nail through his foot—"

"Don't forget the man who came in with a chunk of metal embedded in his eye," Long said. "He thought he was dying. The electromagnet in Ophthalmology took it out, neat as could be."

"And then, of course," Nurse Potter said, "there was the knife case. I've seen a lot in two years on Emergency, but that man lost more blood than I've ever seen anyone lose and still go on living —" The nurse stopped and frowned. "What's the matter, Tommy? You look pale."

Kildare looked at the boy, who was silently sitting on a chair near Nurse Potter's desk. He *did* look pale.

"I'm all right," Tommy said in a cold tone.

"You're right about that knife case," Long said. "We got the hemorrhaging controlled, but I didn't think that guy would last even long enough for the surgeon on call to get here. But he did. The surgeon did a laparotomy to look for internal bleeding. An hour later the patient was upstairs in bed, getting new blood—"

"Tommy," Nurse Potter interrupted, "are you sure you're all right?"

Kildare looked at him. "Tommy, you do look pale."

"I'm all right," the boy said, almost angrily.

Kildare felt the boy really was sick and was trying to hide it for some reason. Kildare would have tried to get to the root of it, but suddenly there was a deluge of patients on Emergency. Long took the first one, a lobster-hued young man who had overexposed himself at the beach today, and disappeared with him into a treatment room. Cassell rushed to assist an aging man brought in by a worried wife. The man was dizzy and nauseous and was talking with thick and uncertain speech; Kildare suspected he had suffered a small stroke.

Kildare drew a pale boy of about Tommy Benton's age, brought in by an older brother. The boy was complaining of severe continuous pain in the right lower quadrant, an area that Kildare found extremely tender to the touch. It looked like acute appendicitis, but Kildare did not leap to say so without further probing, for last week he had mistaken a gastro-enteritis case for acute appendicitis. But the boy's temperature was a hundred and one, and the white blood count was thirteen thousand. The surgeon on call was notified, and within a few minutes the boy was being admitted to the hospital for an appendectomy.

When Kildare and Tommy came out of the treatment room, the nurse told them that the

police had called to report a bad head-on collision involving four persons on the edge of town. Two ambulances had been dispatched to the scene and could be expected back in about twenty minutes.

In the meantime, other cases were piling up in Emergency. Kildare's next patient was a heart case. The man, severely nauseated from digitalis poisoning, was admitted to the hospital to be kept under observation until the toxic effects of the overdose of digitalis were diminished.

When this case was gone, Kildare noticed that Tommy was even whiter than he had been before. When Kildare looked at him, the boy looked down at his hands, as if he were ashamed of not feeling well. Kildare was just about to speak to him about the matter when a new case came in that required the attention of both him and Dr. Cassell.

It was a little girl of about twelve who was choking severely. She was brought in by her mother who was trembling with fright. The next few minutes were fraught with suspense. Despite her continuous coughing, the little girl did not dislodge whatever was caught in her throat. Soon her coughing was weakening and she was going livid, indicating that she was nearing unconsciousness. Death would follow shortly unless her ability to take oxygen into her lungs was restored. Cassell called for the tracheotomy kit to be made ready, and Nurse Potter sent for the surgeon on call.

Kildare tried to calm the increasingly hysterical mother, who was ushered into the corridor, while Cassell passed his forefinger as far down into the choking girl's throat as possible—searching for the obstruction, which was very likely a piece of food caught over the opening to the larynx. Cassell could not locate the obstruction, and began a tracheotomy just as the little girl lapsed into unconsciousness. Cassell worked quickly and surely, cutting a midline incision into the trachea, an opening by which air could be taken into the lungs by way of an inserted tube. But Cassell had to do artificial respiration before the child began breathing again. She was then sent upstairs to a minor surgery room, where the surgeon on call would locate and remove the obstruction, thereby allowing her to breathe by the normal process again.

Kildare walked over to Tommy, shaking his head. "That was a close one." Kildare stopped. "Tommy, you're trembling. You *are* sick—"

"N-No, I'm not," the boy said nervously. "Just don't worry about me. Worry about your patients."

"But—"

Kildare had no chance to finish, for the ambulances had arrived with the victims of the head-on collision, two men and two women, all of them middle-aged. From the moment they were brought in on stretchers by the ambulance attendants, everyone in Emergency was very busy.

One woman was unconscious, and had been,

according to an attendant, ever since she'd been removed from the wreckage. Cassell thought this suggested a fracture of the skull. After the woman's vital processes were checked, she was wheeled to Emergency's X-ray unit.

The other woman, who was under Kildare's care, was hemorrhaging badly from the occipital artery just behind her ear. Kildare stopped the bleeding by compression with a wedge-shaped pad and tight bandage over the wound, and then carefully examined her for obvious fractures, of which he found none. But he suspected that the woman was going into shock. She was exceptionally pale and she was sweating. Her pulse was soft, faint, and rapid, and her blood pressure low. Kildare decided upon an intravenous infusion of dextran solution to restore her circulating blood and tissue-fluid volumes. The first infusion was done rapidly, in five minutes, and by the time it was finished there was a definite improvement in the woman's circulation. Kildare then began a second infusion to sustain the improvement.

He had an opportunity then to see what was going on with the other accident victims. One of the men had a fractured tibia. Aside from that and a few easily treated abrasions, this man seemed to be in fair shape, though he, too, was soon giving evidence of possibly lapsing into shock. Dr. Cassell accordingly started an intravenous infusion.

The man Dr. Long was handling was in much worse condition. He had a broken nose and he'd lost a great deal of blood from two gaping wounds before Long was able to get the hemorrhaging stopped. He was breathing with difficulty, with the right side of his chest immobile—an almost certain sign that a displaced rib had punctured his lung. But he could not be taken for X-rays until his lost blood had been replaced. Long had sent a sample of his blood to the lab for a cross match, and the results were returned quickly. The man was soon making improvement under a transfusion of whole blood drawn from the hospital blood bank.

It was then that Kildare noticed that Tommy was gone. He asked Nurse Potter if the boy had left any word when he'd gone out.

"No," the nurse said. "He rushed right past me as if I didn't exist. I suppose I should have expected that. I've heard he's not the lovable type—or the loving type either."

Kildare turned away from Nurse Potter with a frown. A possibility had occurred to him, and during the next minute or so it kept adding up in his mind. In a way it seemed an absurd possibility, but if his suspicions were true, then this was a serious matter he could not ignore.

But he did not have time to think about it now. He returned to his patient and found her greatly improved, though she was suffering from a severe case of nerves and was extremely apprehensive over her husband's condition. But her husband had rallied from the transfusion, and although an

X-ray of his chest had confirmed that he was suffering a pneumothorax, Kildare was able to convince her that in all probability the condition
would correct itself after a minor surgical procedure.

Within another half hour, the three conscious
victims of the accident had been put through the
admitting procedure and had been taken to the
Intensive Care Unit for the night. The fourth
victim, the comatose woman, was in the Emergency operating room. Her X-rays had revealed a
severe fracture of the skull, and Dr. Vinson, a
neurosurgeon, was to perform an emergency operation in an attempt to save her life.

It was almost midnight before things slackened
in Emergency to the point where Dr. Kildare
could get away. He walked quickly to the interns'
quarters. By all logic, Tommy Benton should be
in bed at this hour, but Kildare had a feeling he
would not be. And he wasn't. A sliver of light

showed under the door of Room 121.

Kildare knocked and boldly opened the door when there was no answer. Tommy was sitting in a chair beside the window. He looked surprised and annoyed by Kildare's intrusion. He was still as drained of color as he had been hours ago in Emergency.

"You couldn't sleep because you've been worrying, haven't you, Tommy? You've been wondering how you're going to force yourself to go through all those years of medical school and all the rest when you don't really want to."

"I—don't know what you're talking about," Tommy said hesitantly.

"You hid it fairly well on the wards, Tommy— but tonight it showed when you were faced with the severe cases in Emergency. You were afraid. All that blood made you sick. Seeing people badly hurt and possibly dying made you afraid—"

"No," Tommy interrupted. "You're wrong."

"Don't hide from yourself, Tommy. I'm being

blunt because I'm trying to force the truth out of you now to save you from hurt later. A doctor can't be afraid of blood, or afraid of seeing people badly hurt, because that will make him afraid to deal with them—"

"I'm not afraid. You've got it all wrong."

"Tommy, stop lying to yourself. Deep inside you, I don't think you really want to be a doctor. It's no disgrace not to want to be one. It's no disgrace to be afraid of blood and injuries, either. There are a lot of wonderful things to do in this world, and the people who are happy are the ones who do what they're fitted to do. You don't act happy, Tommy, and I think it's because you've talked yourself into thinking you want a career you don't really want."

"You don't know what you're talking about!" The color of anger exploded in Tommy's face, a sudden contrast to the extreme paleness he'd shown before. "I want to be a doctor—a surgeon, like my father—and that's all there is to it." He paused, his color deepening. "You'd just like to get rid of me—and you think that saying all this will just make me give up and go home."

"No, Tommy, believe it or not, I'm thinking of your own good."

"If you're thinking of my own good, just go away and leave me alone."

Kildare hesitated, then went to the door, turning back to face the boy just as he was closing it behind him. "I think you're making a bad mistake refusing to face yourself, Tommy."

But out in the corridor, Dr. Kildare reflected that perhaps he had made a bad mistake, too. He did not think he was wrong about Tommy Benton, but perhaps he had been wrong to approach the boy about this matter in such an outspoken manner. Perhaps he should have waited until he had thought this out more. He had little doubt that Tommy would only be all the more hostile to him now.

8 *The Breaking Point*

Mistake or not, there was no taking it back now, and in the morning, after a lot of thinking about it, Dr. Kildare was glad he had accused Tommy Benton. He was certain his feelings about the boy's were right. In Kildare's view, Tommy's denial last night only confirmed that he was determined to save his pride even if he had to lie to do it. Somehow Kildare had to get across the fact that false pride could ruin a person's happiness. He reopened the matter at breakfast, hoping that a night's rest would let Tommy look at it with better perspective.

But Kildare had hardly started before Tommy interrupted. "How many times do I have to tell you you're wrong? Now just drop it. I'm willing to forget what you said if you'll just forget it."

"So you're willing to forget it." Kildare drew a deep breath. "Tommy, you're far too strong-willed and full of pride to be willing to forget an accusation like the one I've made if there weren't some basis to it."

Tommy didn't answer. He frowned and reddened and then looked down at his hands. The boy was obviously embarrassed, and Kildare was convinced he had struck home.

"All right, then," Kildare said. "We'll take it to Dr. Gillespie."

Tommy looked up sharply. "You'd like to make me look bad in Dr. Gillespie's eyes, wouldn't you?"

"Tommy, only you can make yourself look bad —or good—in Dr. Gillespie's eyes. If I wanted to try to make you look bad, I would go alone to Dr. Gillespie about this. You're going with me. I'll tell him what I think, and then you can deny it, if your conscience will let you."

"I don't see any sense in bothering Dr. Gillespie

about it," said Tommy sullenly.

"We can't let things stay the way they are—with neither of us believing the other." Kildare paused and looked squarely at the boy. "Besides, if you're telling the truth, then there's no reason why you should want to avoid taking the matter to Dr. Gillespie, is there?"

That struck home, too. Tommy didn't answer. He had nothing more to say during breakfast, and very little to say on the wards when Kildare was doing his early rounds. At eleven o'clock they were finally summoned to Gillespie's office in response to Kildare's earlier request.

"All right, Dr. Kildare," Gillespie said. "Obviously you and Tommy have encountered a problem. Please get to the point."

Kildare did, repeating what had happened in Emergency last night and the accusation he had made in Tommy's room afterward.

When Kildare had finished, Gillespie turned his eyes on Tommy. "All right, Tommy, let's hear your side of this matter."

Tommy voiced his denial of Kildare's accusation in strong tones and with such a show of sincerity that it seemed impossible that he could be lying. Kildare had a feeling he had been steeling himself for this all morning so he would not appear nervous in front of Gillespie.

When Tommy had finished, Gillespie rose and went over to the window, his hands behind his back. He was obviously weighing in his mind what had been said and trying to decide fairly who was right.

After a while he turned to Tommy. "If Dr. Kildare is right about this, Tommy, then it's quite true that we should reappraise the question of why you are here. A certain amount of squeamishness and concern in the face of open wounds and bleeding is natural and common. But if it persists, it is, of course, an overwhelming handicap. If the fear of blood is inordinate, as Dr. Kildare thinks it is in your case, then you should be thinking of going into some other field—" He stopped and raised his hand when he saw that Tommy was about to protest. "I don't think further talk about this will decide anything. However, I can think of one way we could possibly settle this without loss of time. It would be an experience that you cannot object to if you were sincere about what you said, Tommy. You've heard of Dr. Quintin, haven't you?"

Tommy nodded. "He's a surgeon here, isn't he?"

"Yes," Gillespie said. "Dr. Quintin served a surgical residency here under your father, Tommy, and I can remember your father predicting a great future for him—a prediction which has since been borne out. This afternoon Dr. Quintin is conducting a lecture on abdominal surgery to be followed by an actual operation." Gillespie looked at Kildare. "I'll arrange to have another intern cover your duties this afternoon. You and Tommy will attend the lecture and the operation.

After that, we will decide on how to treat the matter at hand."

Dr. Gillespie's point was clear, and Kildare thought to himself that the hours spent in General Surgery this afternoon would probably be educational in more ways than one. Dr. Kildare looked at Tommy. The boy had paled considerably. It was plain that he fully understood the significance of the test he was going to be subjected to in a few hours.

Dr. Kildare kept watching Tommy carefully, looking for signs that the suspense was building up intolerably in him, that his nerves were getting the best of him. But by the time they walked into the lecture room in General Surgery that afternoon at two, Tommy had shown no signs of breaking. The only difference in him was that he was even colder to Kildare than usual.

During the lecture Tommy sat attentively while Dr. Quintin gave the background of this afternoon's case to the surgical interns and residents in attendance. The preliminary examination had indicated a tumor in the lower abdomen of the patient—a woman of thirty. Dr. Quintin described the surgical techniques he would apply, highlighting his points with diagrams on the blackboard. There was a period of questions and answers, and then Dr. Quintin and his surgical assistants went to prepare for the operation.

Silently, Kildare and Tommy walked to the big operating amphitheater where the operation would be performed—ironically the one donated in honor of Tommy's father by a grateful patient whose life Dr. Benton had saved. They sat down in one of the front rows of seats that encircled the glass-domed operating area. During the next few minutes, a number of persons—members of the surgical staff, residents and interns on surgical service, and a contingent from the nursing school studying surgical nursing techniques—took seats.

After about ten minutes of waiting, Tommy

fidgeted. "What's taking them so long?"

"This is the age of aseptic surgery, Tommy. They're scrubbing up and getting into their masks. The procedure takes a long time."

Tommy said nothing more during the next few minutes, but Kildare noticed that he shifted his position nervously in his seat several times before the preoperative activities began in the operating area. Then the masked instrument nurse and the circulating nurse entered, followed by one of Dr. Quintin's surgical assistants. The scrub smocks of the nurses and the scrub suit of the doctor were all of the pale green hue substituted years ago for white at Blair to reduce the glare during operations. The circulating nurse made a last-minute check to see that all needed supplies were available while the instrument nurse laid out the operating tools in probable order of use. The surgical assistant checked to make certain that all the machines used for testing the patient's condition during the operation were working properly.

Then Dr. Quintin, his other surgical assistant, and the anesthetist entered, followed shortly by the patient, who was wheeled in on a stretcher cart and gently placed on the operating table. Dr. Quintin smiled and talked to the patient as she was anesthetized. When the anesthesia was effective, sterile drapes were applied to the operative site and the operation began.

Dr. Quintin worked slowly and carefully, in exactly the manner he had described in the lecture room. As he needed instruments, he called quietly for them, and they were delivered to him by the instrument nurse. One of his surgical assistants was at his side, the other across the operating table, facing him. Once in a while Dr. Quintin turned his face and the circulating nurse stepped up with a sponge to dry his brow.

The operation went well from the first, with no fumbling or faltering among the carefully trained crew, and with no dangerous reactions from the patient, whose intake of oxygen was carefully watched and regulated by the anesthetist all the time. Unobtrusively, Kildare kept looking at Tommy for signs of wear. They were increasingly in evidence as the operation neared completion. Tommy was white, and he got whiter. He was stiff in his seat. Kildare had a feeling he was going to be sick at any moment. Kildare looked around and saw Dr. Gillespie standing quietly at the top bank of seats, watching Tommy, waiting for the boy to panic, as Kildare was waiting.

But Tommy did not break. He sat there whitened, but he sat there solidly to the finish. Then he turned to Dr. Kildare and said in a triumphant tone, "You see, you were all wrong."

Later Dr. Kildare sat in Dr. Gillespie's office.

"I know Tommy passed the test of watching the operation without getting sick," Kildare said. "But I think it was a matter of sheer willpower with him."

"You may be right, Dr. Kildare. I saw how pale

the boy was. Then again, it was Tommy's first operation. I've seen grown men go pale at seeing their first one. Perhaps I made a serious mistake in inflicting such a test on him. Even if he had become ill, it really wouldn't have proved that he would continue to react that way to surgery."

Dr. Gillespie's way of treating things with such concise logic could be embarrassing at times. And Kildare felt embarrassed. It must look to Gillespie as if he had made an issue out of nothing at all.

"Dr. Gillespie, I thought—and I still think—that Tommy was and is unsuited to being a doctor, particularly a surgeon. I felt I had to bring the matter to a head."

Gillespie nodded. "Certainly doubts like that should be investigated. Then again, Dr. Kildare, there is such a thing as leaping too fast, on too trivial evidence. Perhaps your distaste for this assignment caused you to—"

"Sir," Kildare interrupted, "I don't feel a distaste for the assignment. It's just that I feel that

I'm unsuitable for it."

"Your feeling has been most obvious," Gillespie said grimly, "and I call your attitude a distaste for the assignment, no matter what you call it. My point is, your distaste for the assignment may have driven you to assume conclusions about Tommy without finding sufficient evidence to support them. Naturally the boy is nervous. Wouldn't you be if you were a teenager surrounded by adults in an environment you weren't used to? Dr. Kildare, I think you've failed to give adequate consideration to how Tommy must feel in his position."

"I don't think I've misjudged him or treated him unfairly." But he did feel a small doubt now. "In any event, sir," he went on, "Tommy will thoroughly resent me now for bringing my suspicions out into the open. I know you'll want to relieve me of this assignment and put—"

"Dr. Kildare," Gillespie interrupted harshly, "you could not be more wrong. Removing you from this assignment would prove nothing but that you find it impossible to handle a sixteen-year-old boy. If such is really the case, then we can have doubts about your capacity for handling patients, too. How you settle the differences between you and Tommy Benton is your problem. But I don't want to hear any more nonsense about your wanting to be relieved of this assignment."

"You won't, sir," Kildare said, almost angrily. "However, I hope you realize you may be doing an injustice to Tommy, keeping us together after what's happened. He'll be just as uncomfortable around me as I will around him."

"Sometimes, Dr. Kildare, it is exceedingly uncomfortable to learn the things in life we must learn. You and Tommy Benton are bound to be educating influences on each other. In the end we can hope it will be to the good of both of you."

Dr. Kildare went out, feeling depressed. He had a heavy feeling that it could not turn out well.

9   *A Change for the Better*

The strain between Dr. Kildare and Tommy Benton deepened as the days passed. Tommy showed his deep resentment in his increasingly colder attitude toward Kildare and in his refusal to discuss anything that did not relate strictly to the training program. Every time Kildare managed to catch the boy's eyes, he found anger burning there. And passing time did not diminish that anger. Kildare wondered if Tommy was waiting for him to apologize, to say that he now knew his suspicions were groundless and that he was sorry he had made an issue over nothing.

Kildare would have been glad to apologize if he had been certain he was wrong. But he was not. He still felt that Tommy Benton was not constitutionally and emotionally made up to be a doctor, even if the boy himself did not know it.

But if Kildare was right, then Tommy Benton was doing a good job of hiding the facts from himself and from others. He was alert on the wards and gave his instructor no opportunity to criticize him. Kildare always watched carefully from the corner of his eye as he changed the patients' dressings, expecting at any moment to see Tommy's eyes turn away from some of the severe wounds. But Tommy's eyes held steady, and Kildare was convinced that the boy was acting, was managing to hide his uneasiness through sheer resolution—with the same kind of hard will that had stopped him from showing his fear at the operation he had witnessed.

Kildare was surprised when Tommy's relations with various persons around the hospital began to get better. The improvement started the first day after that tense scene in Dr. Gillespie's office. After rounds that day, Dr. Murray conducted a critique in the conference room on the new admissions, as he often did. Suprisingly, Tommy, who had never previously opened his mouth during these sessions, had several questions about the prognosis for a new patient suffering from a destructive lesion of the right hip. Murray and Udell took great pains to answer the questions, and the next day, when Tommy came up with more questions, the resident and his assistant again went into detail to satisfy Tommy's curiosity.

"Maybe I misjudged Tommy," Udell said to Kildare the day after that. "He hasn't been so bad lately. He seems more interested now, and not so sour. He even seems to appreciate our efforts to answer his questions."

Nurse Joyner had begun to look at Tommy differently, too.

"Every morning he stops and says hello to me and asks me how I am the minute he gets on the service," she told Kildare. "He never used to do that. Maybe he was just shy at first."

That same day, Kildare ran into Nurse Ashby

from Admitting Service and learned something surprising from her, too.

"Yesterday," she said, "Tommy Benton made a special trip down to see me, and he was as nice as you could ask. He asked me to tell him about the days when I was a surgical nurse under his father, and of course I was glad to tell him about them." She smiled. "I shouldn't have been so quick to judge Tommy that first day, Dr. Kildare. I'm sure now that it was just shyness, and not unfriendliness, that made him seem a little strange."

There were more stories around the hospital about the change in Tommy Benton, and Harriman had one of them. He told Kildare that Tommy had greeted him with a smile and a friendly hello in the corridor that day.

"A decided change from the frost he showed when you introduced us in the cafeteria. What kind of magic wand did you wave to do the trick?"

"I'm afraid I can't take credit for it," Kildare told him.

No, he did not see how he could, although his comments to Tommy had possibly given the boy insight as to how the people around Blair really felt about him and had caused him to try to do something about his unpopularity. Or perhaps it was all an act with the boy—an effort to make Dr. Gillespie believe his attitude had changed when it had not really changed at all.

How was Kildare to know whether Tommy was sincere or not? He did not know of any way to find out except to wait. If this was all an act with Tommy, it was bound to show in time. But if it was not an act, if the emerging Tommy was the true Tommy, then Kildare would be glad to admit that he had been wrong about some things.

"I'm glad you're feeling more at home around here," Kildare said to Tommy one day as they came off the last rounds of the afternoon.

It was the first personal remark Kildare had made to Tommy in days, and it seemed to catch the boy off balance. He looked at Kildare in surprise, then quickly looked away.

"I don't know what you mean," he said.

"I think you do. Your attitude toward the people around Blair has been changing for the better, and theirs has accordingly changed toward you, for that sort of thing works both ways. Most people are willing to like you if you're willing to like them."

Kildare hoped that Tommy had caught his hint and that the boy would throw him the rope he had been throwing to some others around the hospital. But Tommy did not even answer. He only flushed, as if he were ashamed of being caught acting human toward others, and then he walked away.

Tommy's attitude was not only changing toward Blair's medical personnel, but also toward the patients. He took more interest in all of them than he had, and the special relationship he had previously established with Henry Reeves, the burn victim, continued to grow. Whenever Kildare and Tommy were near Reeves's small room in the first section of Ward G, Tommy invariably stopped in for a few words with the big man who lay in bed swathed in bandages.

In Kildare's opinion, Tommy could not have chosen a more needful person than Henry Reeves to show interest in. Reeves, with twenty per cent of his skin area deeply burned, with his entire family wiped out, had wanted to die, and there had been fear during the early days of his hospitalization—when he had lain in shock in the Intensive Care Unit—that his death wish would be granted. He was now out of danger from a physical viewpoint, but Dr. Murray was much concerned about his psychological outlook. Reeves continued to be extremely despondent, so much so that shortly after he came on the ward Murray had had him moved from his room to a six-bed unit in the hope that the man would feel more cheerful in the midst of other patients. But the other patients were not much influence on him. Tommy Benton was. Tommy was the only person around Blair who could pull a smile out of Reeves.

And then one day Kildare found out why. On his way through the ward alone, he noticed Reeves staring at him, and he stopped to see if he could do anything to make Reeves more comfortable. Reeves's case had reached the point of simple supportive treatment. It would take time before his condition improved enough so that the plastic surgeon could perform skin grafts on portions of his neck, chest, and arms.

"No, I don't need anything," Reeves said. "Where's Tommy today?"

"Right now he's attending a lecture over in General Surgery."

"Nice boy. He's very proud of what his father did here."

"Yes."

"It must have been hard on the boy, growing up without a father. He said he was only six when his father was killed."

"Yes." Kildare looked at the big man, wondering what his secret was in getting Tommy to talk so freely.

"You know," Reeves said, "my son wanted to be a doctor, too. And he was sixteen—just like Tommy."

That explained it, and after thinking a lot about it, Kildare went to Tommy's room early that evening. The door was ajar, and he knocked and stepped in before Tommy saw him and had a chance to offer any objections. Tommy was dressed in a sport shirt and slacks, and he was combing his hair, apparently getting ready to go out. Kildare was still curious about where the boy went every evening, but he knew that asking about it would bring only a misleading answer or no answer at all.

"Tommy," Kildare said, when Tommy turned to face him with hostile eyes, "I know that things haven't been good between us lately—"

"That's your fault, Dr. Kildare," Tommy interrupted.

"Maybe so, Tommy—though usually it takes two to make things this bad." He paused. "But we won't talk about that, because I don't think either of us is ready to talk about it yet. I came to talk to you about your influence on Mr. Reeves."

Tommy frowned. "I haven't done anything to him."

"You've done a great deal *for* him. Your chats with him have helped him a great deal—and I'm here to ask you to stop and talk to him even more often than you have been. Your talks are doing him as much good as any medical treatment we can offer him. I think he's substituted you for the son he lost in the fire, Tommy."

Tommy looked perplexed. "I don't understand."

"Think about it. One day Mr. Reeves was a happy man with a fine family. The next day he was alone in the world. It's little wonder he almost

died from the shock to his nervous system. He's still depressed and unwilling to face the fact that the world must go on for him, that he must adjust to facing the future alone. That's where you can help."

"I don't know what you mean."

"You can help by being a kind of substitute son for a while, as he wants you to be—and by showing even more interest in him. You've helped a lot already. You may be almost entirely responsible for getting him over the top of the psychological wall he's got to climb before he can leave the hospital and take up his life again."

"I'll help all I can. I would have done it anyway, without your telling me. I like Mr. Reeves."

Tommy went out then, and it was much later in the evening when it occurred to Dr. Kildare that perhaps his theory about the Reeves case worked both ways. It was quite plain that Henry Reeves had substituted Tommy Benton for his dead son. But couldn't it be that Tommy had made a substitute, too? There was quite a resemblance between the big man wrapped in dressings in Ward G and that other man looking down from the huge portrait hanging in Blair's main entrance hall. Yes, Henry Reeves and Dr. Richard Benton looked enough alike to have been brothers.

The girl's name was Betty Norden. She was sixteen years old, very pretty, and extremely nervous. During that first examination in Betty's room in the Private Service wing, her parents fussed so badly that Dr. Kildare was immediately convinced that they were responsible for most of her nervousness.

After the examination, Dr. Yates, the attending physician who was responsible for Betty's being in Blair, held a critique in the Private Service office. Dr. Gillespie was present because Dr. Yates had asked him to examine the patient and had indicated that this was going to be a special case. Dr. Kildare and Tommy Benton were present because Betty had been assigned as one of Kildare's Private Service cases.

"Of course," Yates said, "I can't be positive until all the tests are completed, but I think that Betty's trouble is a congenital heart anomaly—probably tetralogy of Fallot."

Gillespie frowned. "But Betty's a little old for a congenital condition to be coming to light now, isn't she?"

"I think," Yates said, "it would have come to light long ago if Betty had been subject to the normal care of a physician most children have in the course of their childhood and adolescence. But Betty's parents don't believe in doctors. It seems that Mrs. Norden's brother died on the operating table, and they've been taking it out on the whole medical profession ever since. They have Betty scared to death."

"I'm surprised you got her here to the hospital," Gillespie said.

"I wouldn't even have found out about her case

if she hadn't fainted at school one day. I was called by the school nurse. I suspected the congenital condition when I saw that Betty's growth seemed retarded—you saw how small she is—and learned that she's subject to excessive fatigue at the slightest exertion. I contacted Mr. and Mrs. Norden about my suspicions, and they made me immediately aware of their distrust of doctors. I'm afraid I rather threatened them. I led them to believe that unless they permitted Betty to come into the hospital for a thorough examination, I might go to the juvenile authorities about the matter."

"I see," Gillespie said. "I suppose you expect trouble in getting permission for an operation in case Betty's tests turn out positive."

Yates sighed. "Yes. That's why I wanted you in on this from the beginning, Leonard. I have a feeling that if Betty Norden is to be given a chance to grow up and live to a ripe old age, it's going to take all of us to help her do it."

Dr. Yates looked at Dr. Kildare and Tommy Benton. He was including them, too.

Blair General Hospital had a generous schedule for visiting hours, and Dr. Kildare agreed with Dr. Gillespie's philosophy on the matter—that visitors often helped the patients to get well faster, so the more visiting, the better. But in the Norden case, Kildare soon felt that if there were less visiting, the patient would be far better off.

Mr. and Mrs. Norden were nice people, and they were very much concerned about their daughter, and they were in their daughter's room every minute of the day that hospital visiting rules allowed. Plainly, they felt that their presence and the things they said were helping Betty. Kildare was convinced they were having the opposite effect.

"We never should have let Dr. Yates talk us into letting you come here, Betty," Kildare heard Mrs. Norden say one day as he entered the room.

"If they do one little thing you don't like, you just tell them we'll take you right out of here."

Kildare was amazed at the Nordens' attitude, and he would have liked arguing it out with them, but he knew that such an approach would bring severe reproval from Dr. Gillespie, and would do nothing to change the Nordens' deep-seated resentment against doctors and hospitals.

They planted their resentment more deeply in their daughter's mind every day, and their badgering aggravated her bad psychological condition. The beginning tests were simple ones, but Betty had a severe case of the trembles just from having her chest X-rayed. She fainted from fear when a blood sample was drawn from her finger for a count, and she wept so heavily after she was revived that Dr. Gillespie ordered that she be given a day or so of complete rest before the tests continued.

"We can only hope," Gillespie told Kildare, "that we can build up her courage a little by trying to get her to relax. The cardiac catheterization is a difficult test unless the patient is psychologically able to take it."

But the Nordens continued nagging their daughter, and Kildare would have had no hope that Betty would be able to finish the cycle of tests if it had not been for Tommy. Betty and Tommy took an immediate liking to each other, and Kildare was soon aware that Tommy was making special trips to her room to talk to her when her parents weren't there. The two young persons were obviously a happy influence on each other. Twice Kildare walked in and found them laughing. It seemed strange to hear Tommy Benton laugh wholeheartedly, and equally strange to find that the nervous Betty Norden could show some joy in life. Of course, when Kildare thought it over, it seemed perfectly logical that Tommy and Betty had found each other's company agreeable. They were the same age, they were both attractive, and they probably had many interests in common.

"I think you're doing Betty a world of good," Kildare said to Tommy the fourth day Betty was in the hospital.

Tommy flushed. "I like to talk to her. She's a nice girl."

"I think the talks you're having with her are making her less afraid of the hospital—and of us. Dr. Gillespie thinks so, too. We're going on with the tests tomorrow. We think Betty is ready now."

Tommy nodded and seemed about to leave, but Kildare stopped him. He did not think this subject, which he had been thinking about a great deal, should be avoided any longer.

"Tommy, a few days ago I told you I didn't think we were ready to talk about you and me yet. I think we are now. Your attitude toward a lot of people around Blair has improved a great deal, but our relationship doesn't get any better. We spend eight or nine hours together every day. Don't you think we ought to make those hours as comfortable for each other as possible?"

"You'd like me to forget you tried to get me in trouble with Dr. Gillespie by telling him lies about me, wouldn't you?" Tommy asked sharply.

"I only told him—in your presence—what I thought was true."

"You *still* think those things are true! I can tell!"

"I'm not convinced I was wrong. However, I'm willing to let you show me I was. But neither of us can show the other anything at all if we can't communicate with each other."

"You might as well get it straight right now that I could never trust you after what you did to me!" Tommy said with a burst of color spreading over his face. "It's too bad I make you uncomfortable —but it seems to me that's all your own fault!"

The boy wheeled and walked away, leaving Dr. Kildare with clenched fists and a feeling that there was absolutely nothing to be done about altering this clash of personalities.

10   *A Flat Refusal*

The booklet was entitled *Disaster Procedure,* and the original version had been written fifteen years ago by Leonard Gillespie and Richard Benton when the two doctors had established the Disaster Unit in Blair General Hospital. Since then the booklet had been revised many times by Dr. Gillespie to incorporate improved methods learned through experience in answering calls.

Every intern, resident, and nurse in Blair had a copy of the booklet, and they were all expected to know the procedure thoroughly. Gillespie had made it clear that no indecision would be tolerated in answering a disaster call, during which quick action was always necessary for success.

The disaster complement—which included seven doctors, five nurses, and six general helpers

—was rotated monthly, and Dr. Kildare's name had appeared on the new list that had come out yesterday. Accordingly, he had sat down last night to review the booklet thoroughly. He wanted to be completely prepared.

Tommy Benton was carrying his copy of the booklet clutched tightly at his side as he and Kildare walked along the corridor toward the big conference room adjoining Dr. Gillespie's office.

"What did you think of the booklet?" Kildare ventured.

The boy didn't look at him. "It seemed to cover everything that could come up in a disaster," he said in his usual cold tone.

"Yes," Kildare said. "And Dr. Gillespie is right in insisting that we keep up on the procedure. There aren't many disasters, fortunately, but because there aren't we don't get much actual experience in dealing with them. That's why Dr. Gillespie reviews the procedure with each new disaster complement."

They entered the conference room and found two doctors already there. By two minutes of nine, the whole disaster complement was gathered, for no one risked being late when Gillespie called a conference. The older doctor came in at one minute of nine, sat down at the head of the long conference table, and began.

"The Disaster Unit," he said, "renders one of the most important services Blair General Hospital has fostered in this community. In the years since we adopted our disaster procedure, most other hospitals in the area have established disaster teams, too. It's impossible to calculate how many lives have been saved by these teams, but I have no doubt that the number is high. Blair has sent its team to the scenes of railroad accidents, airliner crashes, big fires, explosions, floods, and other catastrophes. Some of you were here last year when our disaster team worked in the midst of the tornado that struck our suburban communities. We don't know what will be next, or when it will come, but whatever it is, and whenever it comes, we intend being ready for it.

"When you see Code two hundred flash on the call box, you report immediately to the dispatch office, where the disaster supplies and equipment will be in the process of being loaded. You will be rushed to the disaster site under police escort, and there you will work from your emergency bags until the supply truck can be unloaded. In the meantime, here at the hospital all doctors and nurses not on duty on the wards will report to Emergency to handle patients sent in by ambulances from the disaster scene. And remember," Gillespie emphasized, "that time is of the essence. We'll be having a disaster drill soon to see how fast you are at getting the job started."

There was a drill that very day. At three o'clock in the afternoon, when Kildare was busy revising order sheets to incorporate the changes Murray had directed after the afternoon rounds, he glanced up at the call box over the nurses' station and saw Code 200 flashing there.

"Come on, Tommy," he said, handing the order books to the nurse as he turned to hurry down the corridor, with Tommy following him. They went down the fire stairs, the quickest way to the ground floor, and reached the dispatch office within two minutes. One other doctor and two nurses on the complement were already there, and Dr. Gillespie was on hand, checking on everyone and everything. The drill was going full scale. Attendants were rolling stretcher carts containing emer-

gency medical supplies and equipment to the supply truck waiting at the curb for a drill loading. Two ambulances and the three station wagons used for transporting the disaster complement waited with engines running.

An orderly handed Kildare an emergency bag. He checked it. Everything was there—drugs, hypodermic needles, rubber gloves, plasma, bandages, and sutures. By the time Kildare closed the bag, the last doctor on the complement had appeared, and Dr. Gillespie looked at his watch.

"You did that in good time," he said. "But, of course, I will expect an even quicker response next time."

Dr. Kildare smiled. Dr. Gillespie was always making it plain that he expected something better next time. And he usually got it.

Dr. Yates's prediction had come true. The X-rays, blood counts, and fluoroscopic studies of Betty Norden pointed to one thing, and the heart catheterization performed on the girl gave the final verification. Betty was suffering from tetralogy of Fallot, a congenital heart malformation. The main artery in her heart was not in its proper position, and there was a defective area in the heart wall.

Dr. Gillespie frowned up at Dr. Kildare from the reports attached to Betty's chart. "The operation Betty needs involves the surgical construction of an artificial shunt between the pulmonary artery and a subclavian artery to allow an increase in the flow of blood through the lung. A delicate procedure, but there is every chance for success in Betty's case in spite of the fact that her symptoms should have been heeded long ago. Dr. Rogers, one of the top specialists in open chest surgery in the country, has examined Betty at my request and is willing to do the operation. But Mr. and Mrs. Norden will not sign the release."

"But don't they understand that Betty's life may depend on this?"

Gillespie shook his head. "I've explained it to them, and so has Dr. Yates, but they prefer to believe we are wrong. The fact that Mrs. Norden's brother died on the operating table is still paramount in their minds, and they won't hear of surgery for Betty. In fact, they want to take Betty out of the hospital right now. I've succeeded in having her retained only by telling them she must have some recuperative rest here before she goes home. At best we have only a few days to convince Betty that the operation is imperative and hope that she will be able to convince her parents in turn. But because of the fear her parents have implanted in her, Betty is more terrified of the idea of having an operation than she is of the possible consequences of not having one."

"Maybe Tommy could help," Kildare said.

Gillespie raised his brows quizzically. "In what way?"

"You know how friendly he and Betty are. Maybe he would be willing to try to influence her.

Of course, it would be an unusual approach."

"Dr. Kildare, at Blair we reject no approach that offers a possibility of positive results, as long as it is an honorable approach. Please talk to Tommy about it right away."

Kildare did. And he watched the alarm grow in the boy's eyes as he listened. By the time Kildare was finished, Tommy was frowning deeply.

"Why are you trying to get me involved in this?" he asked sharply. "Why did you even have to suggest such a thing to Dr. Gillespie?"

"Why, I naturally thought you would want to help since you and Betty have become such good friends," Kildare said.

"Even if I could talk her into the operation, I wouldn't. It isn't my responsibility. I'm here to observe—not to do your job for you."

"Tommy, if I could influence Betty on this, I would be in her room doing it right this minute."

"Suppose I talked her into the operation and she died from it?" Tommy stopped, paling, and for a moment his whole body seemed to tremble. "If that happened, I'd be responsible, in a way."

"What if she dies prematurely because she doesn't have the operation, Tommy? Will you hold yourself responsible then?"

"That's—different," Tommy said hesitantly.

"Tommy, there's always a risk in operations. You expect to be a surgeon some day, don't you? How do you hope to be one if you're afraid to take risks, and afraid to influence patients to have the surgery they need?"

Tommy seemed to tremble all over again. "Don't worry about that. When I'm a surgeon, I'll do the job right—the way my father did his job. But I'm not saying one word to Betty about what she should or should not do—and I don't want to hear anything more about it."

The boy walked swiftly off, his anger reflected in the stiffness of his movements. Dr. Kildare stared after him with a frown. The more he talked to Tommy Benton, the less he understood him.

11 *Almost Friends*

Dr. Gillespie turned just slightly in his chair, as if he could focus his attention even more directly on Dr. Kildare that way. The intelligent eyes pierced Kildare's, and there was a frown overlying them. Kildare fidgeted. What had Tommy Benton told Dr. Gillespie in the hour here?

"Of course," Gillespie said, "I, too, am sorry Tommy has refused to help us with Betty Norden. But his reasons are logical, from his point of view. Perhaps we overstepped in asking him to help."

"I don't think so. He claims to want to be a doctor, but he certainly doesn't look at things from a doctor's viewpoint. What good doctor would avoid trying to persuade a patient to have an imperative operation?"

"You're still not convinced that Tommy ought

to aim for a career in medicine, are you?"

Kildare shook his head. "I don't think he's right for it, or it for him. I've been waiting for him to prove I'm wrong, but I don't think he'll do it. You can go only so far in lying to yourself."

"I'm wondering, Dr. Kildare, if it might be you who is suffering from self-deception instead of Tommy. As you very well know, I had Tommy in here for a talk just before I called you in. My purpose was to evaluate what progress he has made. I asked him a variety of questions touching on all phases of his training. He missed answering only a few of them correctly. On the basis of the test, I'm convinced that we haven't been wasting our time and Tommy hasn't been wasting his. I would certainly say that he's shown an interest justifying the trouble we've gone to in this program, an interest that belies your theories that he ought not to be a doctor and indeed, in his subconscious, does not even desire to be one."

"Dr. Gillespie, when I was in junior high I had

a great interest in forestry. I read everything there was to be found on the subject. I spent part of a summer in the northern forests with my uncle, who is a botanist. Forestry interested me greatly, and still does, but that doesn't say I should be a forester, does it?"

"No."

"I think," Kildare went on, "that the improvement Tommy has made is a matter of determination on his part more than anything else."

"Perhaps, Dr. Kildare, you're worrying about something that doesn't exist. Perhaps you're trying to save face. Few people like to admit they are wrong. Interns are no exception."

Kildare flushed. "I still don't think I'm wrong, sir."

Gillespie leaned forward, frowning. "Dr. Kildare, after you and Tommy Benton and I had that interesting session in my office several weeks ago, you predicted that you and Tommy would be uncomfortable around each other henceforth.

When I was talking to Tommy a few minutes ago, I asked him some rather leading questions about how things have been going between you. He avoided being led into making any comments."

"All right, I'll tell you why he didn't—and what I think you know anyway. From a professional viewpoint, Tommy and I are getting along well. He's determined to make a good showing, and I couldn't ask for a better student. But from a personal viewpoint, we aren't getting along well at all."

"Then in one way you've succeeded in your assignment, in another you've failed."

Kildare nodded. It was not pleasant to admit failure to Dr. Gillespie, but Kildare knew he would have looked even worse in the great doctor's eyes if he had tried to minimize the truth or deviate from it.

"Perhaps," Gillespie went on, "it would have been better if I'd granted your request to be relieved of the assignment when you asked."

Kildare did not nod this time, but sat stiffly in his chair. It was quite true that he probably would have gotten more out of his internship during the last few weeks if he hadn't had to worry about his relationship with Tommy Benton. Then again, avoiding the challenge would have left a gnawing question in his mind. It was true that he had failed to meet the challenge properly, but he was not inclined to give up quite yet. He was suddenly alarmed that Gillespie might be planning to take him off the assignment at this late stage. If that happened, there would be absolutely no chance of his proving himself.

But Gillespie said, "You still have some time left, Dr. Kildare. I *strongly* suggest that you make the best of it."

Why not? Dr. Kildare asked himself, even though the idea seemed absurd, for surely Tommy would refuse. But Kildare decided he would ask the boy anyway.

"I'm off tomorrow noon for the weekend," Kildare said as he and Tommy came off the ward late Friday afternoon. "I'm going to drive home. I was wondering if you'd like to come along."

Tommy's eyes widened with surprise. "Why—I—" he started, then stopped, reddening, obviously not knowing what to think about this.

"You don't have to decide this minute," Kildare said. "But I'd like to have you come along. I think we could make it a pleasant weekend, if we both try. For one thing, we could agree before we start out not to talk about the hospital or the trouble we've had."

"I don't know, I'll have to think about it," Tommy said, frowning, apparently feeling there must be some trick to this. But that evening he stopped at Kildare's door and said, yes, he would go.

Kildare was glad about the boy's decision. He had conceived this idea as his last hope for improving his relationship with Tommy in the little time left. His theory was that if they got away from Blair—where the pressures were hard on both of them—they might relax and thereby be able to look at each other from a new perspective, perhaps understand each other better.

But suppose Tommy didn't relax but spent the weekend continuing to show Kildare the resentment he constantly exhibited at the hospital? Perhaps they needed a weekend away from each other rather than a weekend together. The strain was telling on both of them, and at no other time in his internship and the hard years in medical school had Kildare felt as exhausted and nervous as he had during the weeks he had spent in the company of Tommy Benton.

Yes, perhaps this idea was a mistake. But Kildare could not retract the invitation without looking foolish, and the next day at noon he found that Tommy hadn't changed his mind about accepting it.

"But remember what you said," Tommy said as they got into Kildare's secondhand convertible.

"We don't talk about the trouble we've had. This weekend we pretend it never happened."

"Agreed," Kildare said.

It was a fine, sunny day and the hour's drive from the city to the small town where Kildare had been born was a pleasant one. Tommy had little to say along the way, but the farther they got from Blair General Hospital, the more the boy relaxed, Kildare noticed. By the time the trip was over, most of the care that so often made him look far older than sixteen had vanished from his face.

"This town reminds me of my own home town," Tommy said as Kildare drove through the old-fashioned square and pointed out the new clinic where a half a dozen doctors of various specialties had gone into group practice. "I mean," Tommy went on, "it's so nice and peaceful here."

Kildare smiled. It looked as if getting away from the pressures was really going to do some good. At least it was starting out that way.

But Tommy turned stiff when they turned into

the driveway of Dr. and Mrs. Stephen Kildare's cheerful white house on Elm Street, a rambling place they had lived in since before Jim Kildare's birth. When Kildare's mother and father came right out of the house to greet them, Tommy seemed to stiffen even more. It occurred to Kildare then that Tommy was probably worried that he had told his parents about their problems. But Kildare's mother rescued Tommy from that misapprehension right away.

"I'm so glad you could come home with Jim," she said, with a big smile for Tommy. "I've been wanting to meet you ever since Jim wrote that you were working together. It sounds as though they've set up a wonderful program for you at Blair, Tommy."

Tommy flushed slightly. "Yes—it's wonderful."

"I've been wanting to meet you, too, Tommy," Dr. Stephen Kildare said. "I'm familiar with the work your father did. In fact, I heard him speak at medical conventions when he was at Blair."

The ice was immediately broken, and Tommy was thoroughly relaxed during the big lunch Mrs. Kildare served in the kitchen. Afterward, Kildare showed Tommy the two rooms at the rear of the house, now a library and a den, that had been Dr. Stephen Kildare's office and his examination room when he had begun his practice.

"When I was eight or nine," Kildare said with a grin, "I used to sneak in here when my father was out on calls and practice doctoring. We had a German shepherd named Betty who served as my patient. Betty probably had an ophthalmoscope shining in her eyes, and a stethoscope probing her chest, more than any other dog in history."

Tommy laughed, and it seemed a genuine laugh. Kildare almost sighed aloud with relief. The chances for this weekend being a success looked better by the minute.

Next he took Tommy back to the square and showed him the handsome suite in the new professional building where Dr. Stephan Kildare practiced with his associate, Dr. Meadows. Kildare smiled as he opened one of the file drawers holding hundreds of medical histories.

"My father's been a family doctor for over thirty years," Kildare said. "A lot of his patients have been with him all that time. In a town like this, you get to know your patients well—they're your friends. Dad's had a wonderful life and a full one. He's often said he wouldn't want any other. He certainly works hard—as hard as anyone at Blair does. House calls and hospital visits in the morning—he's on the staff at County General —office hours in the early afternoon, more house calls in the late afternoon, then office hours in the evening. And more often than not he's called out for an emergency in the middle of the night. But after three decades of it, he still loves it."

"Does he want you to be a family doctor, too?" Tommy asked.

"He wants me to be whatever I decide I want to be," Kildare said. "I certainly don't underrate the importance of the general practitioner, and the need for more of them than we're turning out nowadays. But the new developments in all branches of medicine call for more and more specialists, too—because no man can know it all in all branches. Whatever I decide, I must make the decision before December—the deadline for applying for a residency. If I decide to be a general practitioner like Dad, I'll try for the new General Practice residency Blair is offering. Otherwise, it will be one of the specialties."

It was almost four o'clock in the afternoon when Kildare and Tommy emerged from the office. Kildare drove past the old yellow brick building where he had gone to high school and took the country road out to a large nearby woods where he had often gone camping and hunting as a boy. They took a walk and came upon a group of senior scouts who were bivouacking there for the weekend. The scout leader, a man named Martin Olds, had been in school with Kildare.

"We were just going to have a first-aid demonstration," Olds said. "Maybe you'd help us out."

"I've had plenty of training in it," Kildare said with a laugh. "When I was a boy, I learned first aid from my father. Later I improved upon it when I was a member of this troop. Let's hope I'm even better at it now that I've been to medical school."

For the next half hour, Kildare demonstrated artificial respiration, applying a tourniquet, making and putting on a splint, and the proper methods for treating burns, cuts, bruises, and snakebite. He asked Tommy to assist him, and the boy did well. But Dr. Kildare wondered if Tommy would do so well if these were real emergencies, if real blood were being spilled out here. He tried to push the thought away. He had promised Tommy he would not talk about the trouble they'd had. He should not even be thinking about it.

The next day after church, Dr. Kildare drove Tommy out to the lake three miles from town where they swam until they were exhausted and then climbed onto a float to sun themselves. For a long time they just lay there. Then Tommy turned to Kildare.

"This has been a swell weekend," he said.

Kildare smiled. "I think so, too. I think we understand each other better now. I hope things can be better between us at the hospital from now on."

"I hope so, too. Maybe if we both try. . . ."

"I guess I ought to remind you," Kildare said with another smile. "We agreed not to talk about that this weekend."

"But that was before we knew we would get along so well," Tommy said. "I think we can talk about it now without making more trouble."

"All right, Tommy. We'll talk about anything you want to."

Tommy flushed. "I know I've blamed you for everything, but the truth is, both of us are to blame. You shouldn't have accused me of those things until you were sure, but I've been at fault, too. I know I haven't been easy to get along with. I didn't realize how badly I was acting toward people until just lately—and I've tried to do something about it."

"You've succeeded."

"I want to do better," Tommy said. "I—well, the reason I acted badly was because I was scared at first, and I didn't want anybody to see it. So I kept at arm's length from everybody so nobody would see it."

"Scared? In what way?"

"Of making mistakes."

"But everybody makes mistakes. You're expected to make them."

"I don't think my father ever made a mistake in his whole life," Tommy said in a strange tone. "That's what everybody says."

"That can't be true, Tommy, and you know it."

Tommy looked away, obviously refusing to entertain any possibility that his father had been less than perfect, and Kildare shifted uncomfortably, hoping that his frankness would not cause Tommy to withdraw before they were finished with this.

But Tommy went on. "I was afraid of making mistakes—afraid to open my mouth or make a single move for fear I'd say or do something that might cause someone to try to talk me out of doing what I want to do with my life. Which you tried to do. I admit that I was a little queasy about blood for a while—and the queasiness worried me—but it was never as bad as you thought."

"Tommy, I wish you'd said some of these things a long time ago."

The boy turned and looked at Kildare with pleading eyes. "Dr. Kildare, I've wanted to be a surgeon ever since I was old enough to understand what my father did in this world. My mother wants me to be like him. Everybody in my home town expects me to be like him. And I'm going to be like him! Suppose somebody had tried to take away what you wanted at the very beginning, when you were just starting after it? That's what you tried to do to me by saying I couldn't be a good doctor."

Kildare hesitated. "I felt we had to consider the possibility, Tommy."

"We've still got a few weeks to go together—time enough to make up for the trouble between us. I'm willing to be friends, but we can't unless you tell me you believe me when I say I'm not afraid of wounds or bleeding or anything like that."

Kildare hesitated again. Plainly, Tommy very much wanted him to believe this. And it looked as if the boy really did want to be friends and end the uncomfortable coldness between them.

"All right, Tommy. Since you say it's so, I'm going to believe you."

The boy sighed and extended a hand, which Dr. Kildare shook. Then Dr. Kildare lay back on the float with a slight shiver of guilt. He had lied in order to make a friend. The truth was, he almost believed Tommy Benton, but not quite.

12 *A Real Success*

"Go on, Dr. Kildare," Dr. Gillespie said, leaning forward slightly across his big desk.

Kildare hesitated. In a way, he felt a little guilty about bringing this to Gillespie, for what had happened between him and Tommy Benton over the weekend was a personal matter in many ways. But Gillespie could not be excluded from it; he had been involved in Kildare's and Tommy's relationship from the beginning and would continue to be involved until the end.

"Tommy unburdened himself more and more as the weekend went on," Kildare said. "Of course, I'd known before how much he revered his father, but I didn't realize that he's focused his entire existence on the goal of emulating Dr. Benton."

"I find that understandable and admirable."

Kildare nodded. "I do, too. But I'm afraid Tommy has carried it to extremes. He won't be satisfied if he can't have a spectacular career like his father's. In my opinion, he has set an impossible task for himself."

"I take it you're persisting in your doubts about Tommy in spite of all the evidence there's been to refute your suspicions."

"Yes, sir," Kildare said firmly. "But I lied to Tommy and told him my doubts were gone. It seemed the only way to preserve the gain we made over the weekend. I wanted him to develop confidence in me."

Gillespie nodded. "Perhaps that was wise, Dr. Kildare. I think in this case we can overlook a stretching of principle."

"When we were driving back to the hospital yesterday," Kildare went on, "Tommy talked a lot about his life at home. He's never mixed well. I think he's held himself off from others because of lack of confidence in himself. He's the son of a hero, and he's set up standards he feels he must live up to. He's avoided making close friends in fear that he might make mistakes and not measure up to those standards in their eyes."

"If that's true, then he's showing signs of getting over that personality deficiency, Dr. Kildare. He's certainly mixing better here than he did at first."

"Yes—and we can hope he carries that particular improvement home with him. But I'd feel a lot better if the boy would set a lower goal for himself. I'm afraid he's going to be bitterly unhappy if it turns out he can't be the man his father was."

"Tommy has a big dream, of course—but most of the great achievements in this world have been accomplished by men with big dreams. Still, I understand your point. But I think I see a strength in Tommy Benton that you fail to see. That strength makes him determined to fulfill his dream. That same strength will carry him through if he cannot fulfill it." Gillespie smiled. "Most of us turn out to be less than we expected when we were sixteen, but we adjust to life's disappointments and learn to live with our shortcomings. If Tommy ever faces the need to do that, I think he'll meet it squarely."

Dr. Kildare nodded. He certainly hoped so.

It was a hot, humid evening, and Dr. Kildare was off duty. He was restless, and found that he could not keep settled with a medical journal in his room very long. Neither could he sit very long in the interns' recreation room watching television. He decided to take a walk.

He walked without aim, and for blocks, as he thought about Tommy, about Betty Norden and other patients, about his internship and his hopes for his residency. He was so preoccupied that he was oblivious of where he was going. Then suddenly he turned a corner and was confronted with a sign, RIVER STREET CLINIC, and he was suddenly very much aware of his whereabouts. He had heard a good deal about what went on in this grimy brick building located on the fringe of the River Street district, the most rundown part of town, with block upon block of old tenements and narrow streets crowding upon one another.

Kildare looked for a moment at Dr. Paul Worrell's clinic—a favorite subject of Dr. Gillespie in interns' conferences—and then walked slowly on. Down the block he passed the boys' club that, according to Gillespie, the indefatigable Dr. Worrell was also associated with. Turning the next corner, Kildare stopped short. A few yards up the street, standing in the shadows beyond a courtyard adjoining an old school building, was Tommy Benton! But what was Tommy doing in the River Street district? Surely this wasn't where he spent his evenings, was it?

Kildare walked up to the boy. "Hello, Tommy. This is a surprise."

Tommy looked startled, then gave an uneasy smile. "Yes, I guess it is. I suppose you never expected to run into me here—any more than I expected to run into you." He turned to look at the courtyard again. "I want to see the finish of this. Those two boys have been fighting it out for ten minutes; one of them is bound to give up pretty soon."

Kildare looked into the courtyard, which was crowded with youngsters and teenagers in several groups, some just talking among themselves, others engaged in games and contests. The two tall, wiry boys Tommy was watching were engaged in an earnest combat of strength as they stood with their arms and hands pressed together in an Indian grip, each boy straining to topple his opponent off balance. Behind each combatant stood an expectant group of waiting boys.

"Those are two gangs," Tommy said, "and the boys trying to outdo each other are the leaders. I'll bet the shorter one wins." Hardly were Tommy's words out than the shorter boy suddenly bent the taller one backward. The loser fell with a grunt as the group of boys standing behind the victor cheered. "The boy who won," Tommy went on, "wins two times out of three. Sometimes they box, sometimes they wrestle, and once I saw the gangs pitted against each other in a free-for-all."

"Apparently you come down here to watch them often," Kildare said.

"I found that this is the best part of town to see things going on. More people are out in the streets here than in the other parts of town." Tommy smiled. "I know you've been wondering what I do evenings. I do this. I take walks and watch people living their lives."

"So you come here and watch life from the side-lines. Wouldn't you rather be doing things with people instead of watching them, Tommy?"

"Oh, I like to watch," Tommy said, a little un-surely. "And I told you I've never been very good at getting to know people."

"You've been doing pretty well at Blair lately."

"I hope so. I know I've got to be a better mixer,

and when I go back to school next month I'm going to start making up for lost time." He paused. "My father was a good mixer. He liked everybody, and everybody liked him—and that was one reason he was such a big success."

Kildare nodded but did not comment. He told Tommy he was going back to the hospital, and the boy said he would come along. They walked back past the River Street Clinic.

"The man who is responsible for this clinic— Dr. Paul Worrell—is one of those big successes you admire, Tommy."

"Oh?" Tommy sounded doubtful. "This clinic doesn't look like much."

Kildare smiled. "Not from the outside. But it would be impossible to calculate the value of the work that's been done inside. In a way, Dr. Worrell began the way your father did, but instead of going to India, he did his missionary work right here in the River Street district."

"Oh?" he said again. "I've never heard of him."

"Well, of course he isn't famous on the scale your father was, but he's certainly famous in this neighborhood. I imagine he knew your father."

"How would he have known him?"

"Dr. Worrell was an intern at Blair about fifteen years ago, when your father was Chief of Surgery. When Worrell finished his internship, he came straight down here to practice even though most of his cases were on a charity basis and he had a hard time making ends meet. His philosophy was that doctors should go where they are needed,

and he was the first man to do something about the big medical needs of this neighborhood. He started this clinic on virtually nothing, campaigning personally for funds from the city and from the rich. Gradually he induced some of the top specialists in the city to assist him down here on a rotation basis, giving their services free. The place flourishes now, and it's not only helped this neighborhood greatly—it's also helped to take the burden off some of the hospital clinics around town." Kildare smiled. "And Dr. Worrell's work doesn't end with the clinic and his enormous practice down here. He also devotes a lot of time to the boys' club he helped to establish. Yes, we can certainly call Dr. Worrell a success—and a hero."

"I suppose. But not the way my father was."

"Not in the same way, because the circumstances are different—and so is the scope. But I just wanted you to see that a doctor can be a big success on a small scale."

But the subject of Dr. Worrell was not ended

with them. Ironically, the very next morning Dr. Gillespie stopped them in the corridor to introduce them to a tall thin man with a warm smile and a kind face filled with fatigue. It was Dr. Paul Worrell. His eyes twinkled when Kildare mentioned that he and Tommy had taken an outside look at the River Street Clinic last night.

"Drop down Saturday morning and see us in operation," Worrell said. "And maybe you'd like to come along on the outing our boys' club is having in the country Saturday afternoon. Swimming, baseball, a picnic—the whole works."

Dr. Kildare thought it sounded like a good idea, and so did Tommy Benton.

Henry Reeves was propped up against his pillow reading when Kildare stopped at his bed.

"You don't need my help," Kildare grinned. "I just stopped to say hello."

"I'm glad for the hello," Reeves said, his big and hearty face expanding into a broad smile. "It's a good sign that I don't need your help any more, isn't it? It looks as if the plastic surgeon really fixed me up fine."

Kildare nodded. The grafting of the skin from Henry Reeves's thighs to the deeply burned portions of his neck and chest and arms had gone extremely well.

"I'm hoping for a quick recovery now," Reeves said. "As Tommy has pointed out, I've still got a lot of living to do, and I'd better get at it. I'm eager to get back to work. If a man's busy with work, that's half the battle. Life and circumstances will take care of the rest."

A minute later, as Kildare walked toward Private Service, he thought about how Tommy Benton had helped to change Henry Reeves's psychological outlook. Kildare wished the boy would do the same with Betty Norden. Tommy was helping Betty with the interest he showed in her, but he still refused to try to persuade Betty to have the difficult operation she needed.

When Kildare arrived in the doorway of Betty's room, the pretty blond girl and Tommy did not see him, so intent were they upon each other.

Betty was frowning. "Dr. Yates says I can go home in a day or so, but I'm not so sure I want to go. I hated it here at first, but now I don't think it's so bad. I guess I was just scared at first."

Tommy smiled. "The place scared me, too— at first."

"You know," Betty said in a worried tone, "I wish I were sure my folks are right about this— that I shouldn't have the operation. I wish you'd tell me what you think about it."

Kildare held his breath. Betty was literally asking Tommy to convince her to have the operation.

But Kildare did not have a chance to see if Tommy would respond or not, for at that moment a nurse rushed up to tell him that Code 200 was flashing on the call box.

"Come on, Tommy," Dr. Kildare said quickly. "Disaster call!"

13   *Disaster Call*

When Dr. Kildare and Tommy Benton breathlessly reached the dispatch office, the procedure there was going exactly as it had a few days ago during the disaster drill. The ambulance and station wagons were drawn up at the curb with engines running, and the supply truck was being loaded with supplies and equipment. While Kildare was checking his emergency bag, he heard the approaching sirens of the motorcycle policemen who would cut a quick route for them to the disaster scene. The hospital limousine that would carry Dr. Gillespie pulled up just as the last doctor on the disaster complement arrived at the dispatch office.

"That large dry-cleaning establishment on Mulberry Street has had an explosion and a fire," Gillespie said. "First reports indicate there have been a number of bad injuries. We'll get over there at once. We'll probably be the first disaster team to the site since we're the closest hospital to it."

The doctors, nurses, ambulance attendants, and Tommy Benton got into waiting vehicles, and the procession moved away immediately while the sirens of the police motorcycles in the lead parted traffic on the way. Kildare looked over at Tommy, who sat beside him in the first station wagon, and saw that the boy was drained of color. Kildare supposed Tommy was nervous. If so, it was to be expected. Kildare was not as calm as he looked. This disaster call would probably be an exacting test of how well he could handle himself in situations calling for immediate decisions. Of course, he had been subjected to the same sort of test in Emergency Service, but not on the big scale to be expected today.

"You won't be allowed to help us with the disaster victims, Tommy," Kildare said, "so as soon as we get there, just find a good place inside the police line and stay there to watch us work."

In another minute, the emergency procession had turned the last corner and they moved past a lineup of fire engines to the doomed building in the middle of the block. Things were already well organized, Kildare saw as the disaster vehicles were directed into an area in front of the building that the police had reserved for them. The police had confined a growing crowd of onlookers— drawn to the scene by the billowing of black smoke overhead—to the sidewalks behind barricades at a safe distance, and no unauthorized persons were being permitted inside the area.

Kildare got out the minute the station wagon stopped, but Gillespie had been even quicker getting out of his limousine and was already talking to the fire chief directing the rescue operations. Kildare waved Tommy off to the sidelines beside the supply truck, which was already being unloaded by attendants who would quickly set up tables holding drugs, plasma, bandages, splints, and all other supplies that might possibly be needed. They would also set up treatment tables for intravenous infusions and emergency operating procedures.

As he moved toward Dr. Gillespie, Kildare looked over at a group of about thirty persons who had been concentrated close by in an area a safe distance from the building—obviously a group of employees who had been brought out by firemen or who had made it out on their own. A few were standing, but most of them were sitting or lying on the street, most of them looking dazed. Two policemen were overseeing them.

Gillespie turned from the fire chief to address the disaster team.

"The fire is out and the rescue operations are proceeding as rapidly as possible. The persons who seem to have escaped injury have been taken next door to be examined after we've taken care of those needing immediate attention. We can expect a variety of injuries besides burns and smoke inhalation. The explosion flung a number of persons around, probably causing fractures and lacerations and contusions. There are bound to be some severe shock cases, particularly among the burn victims and those who have been trapped inside the building all this time. The explosion collapsed the second-floor stairway, and the people on the third floor are still being brought out by way of a narrow outside fire escape into the side alley. All right, let's go."

Kildare and the other doctors and the nurses headed immediately for the group of fire victims, some of whom were moaning and crying. Kildare stopped at the first person he came to, a young woman grimacing with fear or pain. A man's handkerchief had been applied as a tourniquet above the elbow of her right arm. Below the elbow, a jagged piece of bone pierced the skin. On her arm were large darkening contusions.

"The explosion flung me against an iron vat,"

the woman said in an unsteady and frightened voice. "I was bleeding so much, I thought I would faint before someone helped me. The firemen who came in after me put that tourniquet on to stop the blood from flowing."

"He did exactly right," Kildare said as he loosened the tourniquet for a moment. There was immediate profuse spurting bleeding in the lower arm, indicating that the radial artery had been cut. "We'll get this bleeding stopped and put temporary splints on your arm. Then we'll send you to the hospital for X-rays and a permanent setting of the bone. Right now, while I'm working on you, you can give the nurse the information we'll need so there won't be any delay in continuing your treatment after you arrive at the hospital."

The woman gave her name and address and other pertinent details the nurse asked for, and the nurse recorded them on the emergency tag while Kildare worked—first giving the woman a shot of meperidine hydrochloride to relieve her

pain, then clamping off the cut artery so the tourniquet could be dispensed with. Next he thoroughly cleaned the wound and applied a sterile dressing. Then he took the temporary splints an attendant had brought him from the supply table and placed one behind the woman's forearm and one before it, securing them to the arm with two bandages, one wrapped around the arm at the wrist, the other above the fracture and below the elbow. Kildare next wrapped a broad forearm sling around the woman's neck to support the splints and injured arm in a protective position. Then he completed the emergency tag, designating his diagnosis and the procedures he had followed so that when the woman arrived at Emergency, the doctors there could refer to the tag and proceed to the next steps without delay or repetition.

The woman was sent to the ambulance in time for her to be included in the first shipment to the hospital. The ambulance moved off loaded with six cases in the tier arrangement used in emergencies.

Kildare looked around for an unattended victim and saw a heavy-set man lying on the ground nearby waiting for help. As Kildare moved toward the man, he noticed that one of the surgeons had just completed a tracheotomy on a burn victim whose head had swollen badly from smoke inhalation. As Kildare passed, the emergency tube had just been inserted into the man's windpipe and he was already breathing more freely.

The supine, heavy-set man was groaning and gritting his teeth when Kildare came up. His right leg was severely lacerated and bruised.

"It was caught under the stairway that collapsed, Doctor."

With the support of a fireman, the man had managed to hobble out of the building after he had been freed from the wreckage, but despite the fact that he seemed to have escaped without fractures, his leg was badly damaged. Kildare felt that any undue delay might necessitate the amputation of the limb. He immediately called for attendants to take the man to an ambulance. Back at Blair, surgeons would perform delicate surgery to sew back together the torn blood vessels in the man's leg before the tissue died.

Blair's second ambulance pulled away just as a disaster unit from another hospital arrived. The new contingent was a welcome addition because firemen were still bringing out new victims from the building every minute. One sobbing woman was handed by a fireman to Kildare while he was on his way from one patient to another.

"It was terrible," she wailed, "waiting in there, trapped upstairs, not knowing if they'd ever get us out! It seemed like hours."

She clung to Kildare's arm and sobbed uncontrollably. He examined her as best he could and did not find any wounds or burns. The woman seemed to be suffering a simple hysterical reaction from her frightening experience inside, and Kildare administered phenobarbital in an attempt to calm her before she was sent on to the hospital.

Kildare's next case was a man suffering burns confined to his arms and neck, the rest of his body seemingly having escaped injury from the flames because of the heavy work clothing he wore. Kildare judged the burns to be of second-degree depth. He injected morphine to ease the man's pain and then he carefully cleaned the burned areas and rinsed them with sterile saline solution. Next he applied sterile gauze bandages.

Before Kildare turned to another patient, he looked over at the supply truck, expecting Tommy to be watching the proceedings from there. But he wasn't. Kildare circled the vicinity with his eyes and didn't find the boy anywhere. But he did not have time to look for him, for he suddenly had a seriously injured patient on his hands. The woman had just been carried down from the third floor by two firemen. She had suffered severe face burns, and she was showing all the signs of advanced shock—low blood pressure, a rapid pulse, cold and clammy hands, a pale face with beads of cold perspiration, and irregular respiration. The woman's state was too serious even to allow the ten-minute delay it would take to get her to the hospital. Kildare had her taken to an empty treatment table where an immediate intravenous infusion to restore her circulation was begun by the doctor and nurse in charge.

Another woman in advanced shock was being treated there, and a man who had hemorrhaged badly was being given a blood transfusion. Kildare paused at the treatment tables long enough to give a sweeping look around for Tommy again, then returned to the group of victims, which was beginning to thin down. But he still attended to several more cases before he was finished—more burns, a leg fracture, another advanced shock case, a smoke-inhalation victim, and a man whose face was embedded with glass splinters from a window that had been shattered by the explosion.

After that, the people next door were checked, and then it was all over. The ambulances had departed for the hospital for the last time, and Kildare was able to take a real look around for Tommy. But the boy was not around.

Frowning and wondering about Tommy's disappearance, Kildare joined the rest of the disaster complement gathered around Dr. Gillespie.

"A good job," Gillespie said. "Every one of you did exactly as I expected you would in a real emergency such as this one has been."

They were dismissed to return to the hospital. Dr. Gillespie did not seem to have noticed Tommy Benton's disappearance, and Dr. Kildare decided to say nothing about it for the moment. Perhaps the boy had simply decided to go back to the hospital early.

But Kildare had a feeling it was something else.

When the disaster complement arrived back at Blair, Emergency Service was crowded with patients who had been initially treated at the disaster site and were receiving further treatment here.

The operation was going as smoothly here as it had at the disaster site, with the doctors and nurses not on ward duty fully turned out at Emergency to handle the heavy influx of admissions. Kildare was not needed, but he looked thoroughly around Emergency for Tommy Benton before he went on to other parts of the hospital to search for the boy. But Tommy was nowhere to be found, and he did not return to the hospital all day.

When Kildare went off duty, he walked down to the River Street district and covered street after street looking for the boy. He finally found him on a lonely dock.

Tommy hung his head when he saw Dr. Kildare.

"I ran away from it because I couldn't face it," he said in a choked voice. "You were right about me all along. I'm a coward!"

14 *Time for Truth*

Dr. Gillespie sat behind his desk, his face more serious than Dr. Kildare had ever seen it before. Dr. Kildare's face was serious, too. Now that it had happened, now that his suspicions about Tommy Benton had been borne out, Kildare did not feel at all triumphant. He could not remember when he had felt more depressed than right now.

But Tommy Benton seemed relieved that the pressures boiling inside him had forced the truth to the surface. It was he who had insisted to Kildare that they go immediately to Dr. Gillespie about it, and it was he who was doing all the talking. It was true, Tommy said, that the sight of blood still made him sick. It was true that the sight of badly hurt persons made him tremble. It was true that the courage he had displayed

185

when he had watched the operation had been only a false show.

"I was sick half the night just thinking about that operation," he said with a deep sigh. "Ever since then I've been worried that something might happen where I wouldn't be able to hide my fears. It happened today. I saw all that blood and all those badly hurt people, and I got panicky—so I ran."

It was finished, and now the boy looked down at his hands. Dr. Gillespie, who had sat forward intently while he listened, now leaned back in his chair.

"Getting the truth out into the open makes you feel a lot better about yourself, doesn't it, Tommy?" Gillespie said in a kind tone.

The boy looked at him. "Yes. But it makes me ashamed, too."

"Ashamed?" Gillespie said. "Everybody's afraid of something, Tommy. Admitting your fears is what takes courage."

"But this means that my whole future is going to be different from what I've always wanted. I can never be a doctor."

Gillespie leaned forward again and smiled at the boy. "Tommy, as a Professor of Medicine, I once served on the admissions committee of the medical school, so I know their procedure. There are always twice as many pre-medical students applying for admission as the medical school can accommodate, so the job of selection is a careful process. The applicant's grades in college and his score on the Medical College Admission Test bear great weight, of course, and the lazy and ignorant students are automatically eliminated. With what a student is subjected to in medical school, he must be not only highly intelligent but also ambitious and energetic if he is to get through the courses. On any of those counts, you would be highly acceptable, Tommy."

"But, Dr. Gillespie—" Tommy began.

"Let me continue," Gillespie said, raising a

hand. "What I've described is only the initial process in the elimination procedure. More applicants are rejected during the personal interview. Admissions committees can usually spot those who are temperamentally unsuited for a medical career. Eliminating them in the beginning can save them a lot of wasted time—and a good deal of despair in later years."

"I guess I fall in that category," Tommy said in a bitter tone. "Temperamentally unsuited to be a doctor."

"One of the questions the committee always asks the applicant," Gillespie went on, "is 'Why do you want to be a doctor?' There are a number of acceptable answers. At the top, of course, is the desire to help the sick. Now, Tommy, if an admissions committee asked you why you want to be a doctor, what would you answer?"

"I'd say that I've dreamed of being one since I was a boy, and have never wanted to be anything else. I think I'd also say that I wanted to be a doctor because my father was one."

"I think those are both good reasons, Tommy," Gillespie said, surprisingly. "But haven't you omitted one of your reasons? Haven't you also wanted to be a doctor because you've entertained dreams of recapturing your father's glory—of being the big man he was?"

"Yes," Tommy said, reddening. "That isn't a good reason, is it?"

"No," Gillespie said.

"It was a stupid dream anyway," Tommy said. "We all know now that I could never be like him if I tried for a thousand years."

"But is it necessary that you be like him?" Gillespie said. "What's wrong with being just yourself, Tommy? Think about it. Would your father want you to be anything but what you are?"

"I don't know. But why talk about it? Everything's over. I'm not going to be a doctor, so why do we have to talk about it any more?"

"Because," Gillespie said, "it isn't sensible to

dispose of a lifetime dream with a few words. Let's go on. Or are you going to hide from yourself again?"

"No," the boy said, drawing himself up. "I'm through with that."

"All right," Gillespie said. "To get back to our admissions committee, after it satisfies itself that an applicant's motive in seeking a medical career is acceptable, it next considers the applicant's capacity for meeting responsibility squarely. A very important aspect. A doctor must constantly be making instantaneous decisions and taking positive action, often on life-and-death matters. His capacity for doing so represents the degree of responsibility he is able to show."

"I certainly would never pass on that question."

"Tommy, you must remember that you've never really faced a situation where you personally had to make a life-and-death decision on the spot. So you don't know how you would react."

"It's easy to guess. I'd probably turn and run."

"I have a feeling you wouldn't, Tommy," Gillespie said.

Tommy looked surprised, and did not answer.

"But let's get on with this," Gillespie said. "Another quality an admissions committee looks for in a prospective doctor is his ability to understand all kinds of people and get along with them. He must be able to inspire their confidence."

"I'm at rock bottom on that count," Tommy said.

"Most of us could stand some improvement in personality aspects," Gillespie said, "and I think you've made great strides in that respect in the few weeks you've been with us. Besides your improved relations with the staff, we must consider the friendships you've developed with Mr. Reeves and Miss Norden."

"But they're special."

Gillespie smiled. "In time, I don't think you would find it hard to make every case a *special* one, Tommy—as all good doctors do."

Tommy frowned slightly. "Dr. Gillespie, it's almost as if you're trying to talk me into going on with my crazy dream to be a doctor."

Gillespie held his smile. "I'm trying to stop you from throwing it all out the window at the pitch of an emotional moment. I have a feeling you're planning to leave Blair soon—perhaps even today."

Tommy flushed. "I was thinking about it."

"I think you should stay around until this has cooled a little, until you've thought it out carefully. You see, Tommy, no doctor is perfect, as you seem to think you must be. A man can be much less than perfect and still be a fine doctor. Certainly the aim of every admissions committee is to select as nearly perfect applicants as possible. But no committee would reject a man with fine leadership qualities just because his grades weren't quite tops. Conversely, a poor mixer would not be rejected if his scholarship was outstanding. Such men often have spectacular careers in medical research. Maybe that sort of thing is what you should be considering instead of aiming for surgery—"

"Oh, no, Dr. Gillespie. I couldn't even consider that!"

"How do you know you couldn't consider it? Have you ever even thought about it?"

Tommy's eyes fell. "No—but—"

"Think about it, Tommy. Think about everything we've said in here before you make a decision. And remember that what we've discussed in here will remain confidential among the three of us. You may go, Tommy."

The boy rose a little uncertainly, his expression a question mark, as if he found it impossible to believe that this had not been the ordeal he had expected. "Yes—I'll think about it, Dr. Gillespie. And thanks."

The moment Tommy Benton had closed the door behind him, Gillespie rose from his desk.

"It would appear, Dr. Kildare, that you were

right about Tommy Benton to a considerable degree from the very first."

"I guess so," Kildare said. "I was hoping I wouldn't be."

Gillespie smiled. "I think I recall that you didn't like Tommy very much at first."

"No, I didn't. But I've changed my mind."

"Circumstances and passing time change many things, Dr. Kildare, and I think we should wait a little longer before we presume to judge what those two elements—plus the influence of some of us around here—have done to Tommy Benton."

It was fine with Dr. Kildare. He wished he'd had more of Dr. Gillespie's patience in this matter all along.

Henry Reeves was propped against his pillows, a slight frown puckering his brow.

"I was really surprised, Dr. Kildare, when the boy said he might be giving it up. He told me he's found he isn't suited to being a doctor. That's the craziest thing I ever heard of, and I told him so. Imagine—he wanted to throw away his big dream just like that!" Reeves snapped his fingers. "He seems to have gotten off the track in his thinking, Dr. Kildare."

"I guess we all do at times, Mr. Reeves."

"Well, I'm trying to get him back on the right track. I think that's what his father would have tried to do." Reeves sighed. "We all reach crossroads where we don't know where to turn, and at those points we need help. I ought to know all about that. And since Tommy helped me pull out of my slump, the least I can do is help him pull out of his."

Kildare smiled at the big man. "That's a fine attitude, Mr. Reeves."

"Fine or not, it's the only kind of attitude I can have, Dr. Kildare. Remember, my son wanted to be a doctor. That won't happen now—but I can hope to live and see Tommy Benton become one some day."

When it happened, it happened very suddenly, and Dr. Gillespie and Dr. Yates were quick to get Mr. and Mrs. Norden to sign the consent to operate before they changed their minds.

"I finally decided," Tommy told Kildare, "that I'd better try to persuade her. It wasn't hard. She really wants the operation, and she was only waiting for me to push her. The best argument I had was that a successful operation will give her a chance to lead a completely normal life. After we talked, she stood up to her parents and said she wouldn't go home with them until she'd had the operation." He smiled. "I think even they have changed their minds a little about hospitals."

"Good," Kildare said. "I'm glad about it."

"I'll feel better after the operation is over and I know whether I can live with a clear conscience."

Kildare knew how Tommy felt. The boy had accepted responsibility he had not had to accept, and that was all to the good as long as nothing went wrong in Operating Suite C, where Dr.

Rogers performed the long and delicate procedure in open chest surgery on Friday morning. Tommy wanted to wait outside the operating suite, but Kildare convinced him he would be better off going on rounds as he usually did.

At eleven Dr. Gillespie arrived on the ward smiling.

"Betty's in the recovery room doing very nicely," he said. "There's every reason to believe there won't be any complications at all."

Tommy drew a sigh of relief.

"Tommy," Gillespie went on, "I'm sure you realize this wouldn't have been possible without your help. You inspired confidence in Betty when the rest of us failed. If you can do it with her, you can do it with others. And it's the hallmark of a good doctor, Tommy."

Tommy smiled, but his eyes were sad. It looked to Dr. Kildare as if the boy welcomed this encouragement from Dr. Gillespie but did not think it made up for some other things.

15 *A Test for Tommy*

Dr. Kildare knew that Tommy Benton had been thinking and had been weighing things, pro and con, all week as Dr. Gillespie had asked him to. But apparently the boy's success in the Betty Norden matter was not enough to change his attitude greatly, for he told Dr. Kildare on Saturday morning, when they were on their way to Dr. Worrell's River Street Clinic, that he thought he would not finish out the last few weeks remaining on his training program at Blair.

"Enough time has been wasted on me as it is," he said.

"Dr. Gillespie doesn't consider it a waste," Kildare said quickly, "and neither do I."

Tommy didn't answer, and Kildare hoped the boy would change his mind. Perhaps this day away from the hospital would sharpen Tommy's perspective, as the weekend away from the hospital at Kildare's home had changed his outlook at another important point.

Certainly the River Street Clinic should inspire Tommy, Kildare thought as they were shown around there—for here was a perfect example of what a dedicated doctor with ambition and energy could build from nothing. It was hard to believe that Dr. Worrell had started alone here in just one room with virtually no equipment. The clinic was now like a small, well-equipped hospital. It bustled with volunteers and social workers as well as the specialists who donated their time.

Worrell smiled as they sat down in his office after the tour of inspection. "When I started here ten years ago, I had to do all the diagnosing myself. Things are much better now. Nothing gets past us, for we have every kind of specialist from internist to dermatologist to neurologist helping us out here."

Kildare asked questions, hoping Tommy would, too, but the boy was silent and rather moody.

He was still silent as they rode out to the country for the boys' club picnic an hour later. He and Kildare were in the lead station wagon along with Dr. Worrell and the River Street district boys who were junior officers of the club. Just as they entered the forest preserve where the outing was to be held, Worrell turned to Kildare.

"I'm always glad to have another doctor along on these outings, Dr. Kildare. Once in a while someone gets hurt. We have first-aid kits and emergency supplies along to meet any unforeseen accident, and of course I have my physician's bag with me."

The picnic area was a grassy open space leading into the forest, with a dirt portion set off for games. A baseball game was proposed at once, and Kildare was asked to umpire. The teams were to be composed of all those not assigned to work details and those not interested in swimming or bird watching. Dr. Worrell assigned six boys to go into the forest to look for firewood and four boys to work at the big stone fireplace where the corn would be roasted and the hamburgers grilled.

"How about playing ball with us?" one of the club's officers asked Tommy.

"Thanks," said Tommy, "but I think I'll sit this one out."

Kildare was a little disappointed that Tommy wasn't mixing when he had the opportunity, and he hoped the boy would join in the game later. But when Kildare looked around for Tommy after the third play of the first inning, the boy was gone. There was only one place he could have gone—into the forest. Kildare hoped he wouldn't get lost in the maze of paths that wound through the preserve.

A few minutes later, when they were deep into the second inning, one of the boys from the firewood crew came plunging out of the forest shouting. The game came to an immediate halt.

"George almost drowned—maybe he's dead by now!" the boy said breathlessly as Kildare and the players gathered around him. "And Carl got his head split open with a hatchet!"

"How did it happen, Eddie?" one of the boys asked, and then all the boys began to ask questions, and they all wanted to run to the scene of the accidents, but Kildare succeeded in quieting them.

"Did you try to do anything for either of the boys?" Kildare asked Eddie.

"That Tommy who came with you is taking care of George—and I think he's helping Carl, too. I don't know. He said to bring help—*quick!*"

Everyone wanted to go, but Kildare convinced the boys that too many at the scene would only create confusion. Kildare sent one boy to look for Dr. Worrell, who had taken a few boys into the forest for bird watching, and then he selected four boys from among the ball players to serve as stretcher bearers if needed. Quickly they gathered blankets, poles, and the physician's bag from the station wagon and were on their way, with Eddie in the lead and Kildare at his side.

On the way, Eddie excitedly related the accidents in greater detail.

"I wandered away from the firewood crew to try to find some fallen limbs, and I heard a shout for help coming from the stream. I ran for the stream, but it was a couple of minutes before I got there, and when I did I found Tommy there diving. I can't swim, so I was no help. Tommy had got there too late to see who was drowning, or where he'd gone down, but he kept diving until he found George and brought him up. Tommy was breathless from all that diving, but it didn't stop him from getting right to work on George. I thought George was dead. But Tommy turned him over and did artificial respiration on him—forever, it seemed like. Then George started to breathe a little, and Tommy told me to run and get you."

Eddie had begun the trip only to run into another accident on the way. He happened into the area where the firewood crew was working, just in time to see one of the boys lose his grip on his hatchet while he was chopping off a limb up in a tree.

"The hatchet," Eddie went on, "dropped right down on Carl's head and split it open. He dropped like a rock, and he was bleeding like crazy. I told Albert to run for Tommy, and then I came straight on for you."

Kildare's heart thumped with excitement. Tommy had shown great courage and responsibility in rescuing the drowning boy and sticking with him until he got him breathing again. But had Tommy's courage held up when he had been confronted with the sight of blood flowing from a split skull?

In another minute, Kildare had the answer to his question. They turned the last bend in the path, and there, in a small clearing, Tommy Ben-

ton was bent over a prostrate boy with an ugly gash in his head.

"You're going to be fine," Tommy was saying to the boy as Kildare rushed up with the physician's bag.

Tommy had certainly done everything he could to save the boy. He had stopped the bleeding— which had been profuse, judging from the large dark spots on the ground where Carl had bled— by finger pressure since he'd had no pressure dressings available.

Kildare sent two of his stretcher crew with Tommy back through the forest to pick up George, and he directed the other two boys to make a stretcher with a blanket and poles while he was giving emergency treatment to Carl. He irrigated Carl's bad wound with isotonic saline from the physician's bag and then did a closure by suture while the boys laid a blanket out on the ground, placed the poles at thirds on it, and then wrapped the blanket tightly around the poles, creating an emergency stretcher. A minute later, the unconscious boy was being carried up the path by his friends. At a fork they met Tommy, who was in the lead of the stretcher crew carrying George.

When they emerged from the forest, they found that Dr. Worrell had just returned with the boy who had been sent to look for him. He gave a low whistle when he heard what had happened.

"I'm certainly glad you two accepted my invitation to come along today," he said, looking at Kildare, then at Tommy Benton.

An hour later, after the accident victims had been taken in to Blair by station wagon and treated in Emergency, Kildare finally had a moment alone with Tommy and was able to say what he had been thinking ever since he had seen the boy bending over the injured Carl in the forest.

"You acted like a doctor today, Tommy. You were faced with sudden responsibility, and you met it squarely. Dr. Gillespie was right. He thought you would come through when the test presented itself, and you did."

"But I acted before I had time to think and get scared," Tommy said with a little frown. "I wonder if I can do it again."

"Sure you can do it again. You're over the hurdle, Tommy." Dr. Kildare smiled. "I'm sure you're going to be a very good doctor."

On the first of May the following year, eight months after Tommy Benton had left Blair General Hospital, he was due back for the dedication ceremony of the new Benton Surgical Research Pavilion.

Ten minutes before the ceremony was to begin in the new pavilion's assembly room, Dr. Kildare stood outside the double doors looking at his watch and wondering if the boy had changed his mind.

At that moment, Tommy came around the corner, grinning broadly when he saw Kildare, quickening his step and coming up with an extended hand. As Kildare smiled back and shook the eager hand, it occurred to him that this was a complete contrast to the first time he had shaken Tommy Benton's hand—that day last July when a surly, frightened boy had barely acknowledged their introduction and had whipped his hand away.

"You look different, Tommy."

It was true. The boy looked taller and a little heavier. And he looked happy and confident, even more so than he had last September when, on his last day at Blair, Dr. Gillespie and Dr. Kildare had told him that he had made the junior intern program a complete success.

"I'm older, Dr. Kildare, and maybe a little wiser. And I've had a good year at school, as I wrote you."

Tommy had written often since he had left, and his letters had radiated his happiness. He was doing very well in school his senior year, and he had made a lot of new friends simply by being himself and mixing well. Kildare supposed that a lot of people had been surprised at the new Tommy Benton. What they probably did not realize was that the new one had been inside the old one all the time, waiting to emerge.

"You look different, too, Dr. Kildare."

Kildare smiled. "I'm older, too. And I've been through a half dozen more services since you left here, so let's hope I'm a little wiser."

Tommy laughed. "I just saw Mr. Reeves."

"Oh, so that's why you came skidding in here at the last minute."

Tommy nodded. "We had a lot to talk about, even though we've been writing steadily. He's coming along fine—busy on the job and off. He's helping Dr. Worrell with his boys' club, as we hinted he ought to. He's too busy to be unhappy."

"What about Betty?"

Tommy's color deepened a little as he grinned. "I'm stopping to see her before I take the train home. But I already know she's fine. We've been writing. She's going to State this fall, so I suppose we'll be seeing something of each other there."

Kildare smiled to himself. He supposed they would, too.

They went into the assembly room, which was soon filled with members of the surgical staff, members of the board, representatives from the Medical Association, and old friends of Dr. Richard Benton from around Blair General Hospital and the city. Dr. Gillespie came in, nodded at Tommy with a smile, and made a fine dedication speech that reviewed the rich accomplishments of Dr. Benton in his service to Blair General Hospital and to mankind in general.

Afterward, Kildare went around the hospital with Tommy while the boy said hello to doctors and nurses he had known during his training as a junior intern. Everyone from Nurse Ashby right up through interns Harriman and Franks was glad to see him, although Kildare could remember a time when this would certainly not have been the case.

The last stop was at Dr. Gillespie's office.

"What about the future, Tommy?" Gillespie asked.

"Still the same dream," Tommy said, "but it's down to earth now. My father was a wonderful man, and I'd like to be just like him, but if I can't, that doesn't mean I can't be a good doctor."

Gillespie smiled. "I'm sure that no matter what you end up being—surgeon, general practitioner, medical researcher, or whatever—you're going to be among the very best in your field, Tommy."

Dr. Kildare thought so, too, and a half hour later, after he had said good-bye to Tommy Benton, junior intern and future Doctor of Medicine, he stood for a long minute and looked up at the huge portrait of Dr. Richard Benton hanging in Blair's main entrance hall. Dr. Kildare had a strong feeling that Dr. Benton would be very proud of the way his son had turned out.

Whitman ADVENTURE and MYSTERY Books

Adventure Stories for GIRLS and BOYS...

TIMBER TRAIL RIDERS
The Long Trail North
The Texas Tenderfoot
The Luck of Black Diamond
Mystery of the Hollywood Horse
The Mysterious Dude

POWER BOYS SERIES
The Haunted Skyscraper
The Flying Skeleton

DONNA PARKER
In Hollywood
At Cherrydale
Special Agent
On Her Own
A Spring to Remember
Mystery at Arawak
Takes a Giant Step

TROY NESBIT SERIES
Sand Dune Pony
Diamond Cave Mystery
Indian Mummy Mystery
Mystery at Rustlers' Fort

New Stories About Your Television Favorites...

Dr. Kildare
Assigned to Trouble
The Magic Key

Janet Lennon at Camp Calamity

Walt Disney's Annette
Mystery at Smugglers' Cove
Desert Inn Mystery
Sierra Summer
Mystery at Moonstone Bay
Mystery at Medicine Wheel

Combat! The Counterattack

The Beverly Hillbillies

Lassie
Secret of the Summer
Forbidden Valley
Mystery at Blackberry Bog

Lucy and the Madcap Mystery

Patty Duke and Mystery Mansion